SHATTERED TRUST

MAIL ORDER BRIDES OF SPRING WATER
BOOK TWO

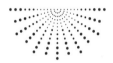

KATHLEEN BALL

I dedicate this book to my son Steven. He's a hard worker and he's such a good father to his daughter Mavis. I'm very proud of him. And as always to Bruce, Steven, Clara, Colt, Emery and Mavis because I love them.

CHAPTER ONE

arker smiled as he stared down at the baby sleeping in his wooden cradle. Douglas Parker Eastman, his son. The baby had dark hair and lots of it. In his opinion his son looked just like him. With a bit of reluctance, he turned from the cradle and took a seat on the sofa next to his wife, Georgie. Gently, he put his arm around her.

"Best thing I've ever done, having a son."

She elbowed him in the ribs. "I think I deserve the credit. I did all the hard work." She leaned over and kissed his cheek. "You're still going to talk to them, aren't you?"

He shifted his weight a few times, trying to find a comfortable spot. "Are you sure it's a good idea? I mean I really don't want to get involved in the men's personal lives."

"Yes, but Douglas will need playmates, and just think we could have a school right here on the ranch if we had more children on it."

Parker found it near impossible to say no to Georgie. "Well, so far we have a grand total of one child. I don't see as your plan will make a difference."

"I wouldn't mind a few more females around to talk to.

You can't let your friends stay lonely. You'll be doing them a favor." Her smile lit up the room. "Now go on and have your meeting. I'll want details when you get back."

Parker stood and opened the door. He glanced over his shoulder at his beautiful blond wife. She wanted the ranch to become more of a community. He had a sneaking suspicion she wanted to build a town on his land. There were too many northerners in the nearby town of Spring Water for her taste. She still woke up screaming at times. The civil war had been hard on most folks, and she was no exception.

He sighed and went into the barn to meet with three of his men. They stood as soon as he walked in.

"Sit, we aren't in the army anymore. Actually, you might want to hear what I have to say sitting down anyway."

The three men before him had followed him into every battle, and they had a bond that hadn't been broken. Sergeant Austin Maxwell, Corporal Kent Sandler and Corporal Lex Willis were the best friends a man could have.

Parker paced back and forth for a minute. The he stood still. There was no reason to drag it out. "Georgie wants more children."

Willis turned red. "I'm not sure that's something we can help you with, Captain. You did just fine with your first one."

Parker waved his hand. "Let me start again. Georgie would like for you to find wives." He smiled at the down-hearted expressions on their faces. "As an incentive, whoever gets married first will have a house built."

Sandler narrowed his eyes. "Built where?"

"Close enough you can walk to the barn. Georgie wants to build a community of families."

Maxwell scowled. "No offense to your wife, Captain but why do we have to do what Georgie, says? We've gotten along well enough without interfering women around. I'm not saying that your wife is interfering. I'm not even sure there's a lady in town I even like."

Sandler jumped up. "I'm going to town and I'll bring back a bride. I always wanted a house of my own." He ran out of the barn and quickly mounted his saddled horse and was off.

"Figures Sandler wants to get to town first. He always wants to win," Willis practically growled.

Parker laughed. "Just because he gets to town first doesn't mean he'll find a bride first. You have to court a woman, ask for her hand in marriage and plan a wedding. I think this is anyone's house to win."

Willis started for the door. "I know a short cut."

Maxwell and Parker exchanged grins.

"Aren't you going to town?" Parker asked.

Maxwell shrugged. "In everything you want to win, there must be a plan. I'm going to the bunkhouse and think about this for a bit."

Parker watched Maxwell walk to the bunkhouse as if he was out for a stroll. He wasn't hurrying a bit. What was Maxwell up to?"

CHAPTER TWO

*T*wo weeks later, Veronica Nolan righted her green hat, held on tight to the bundle she carried, and exited the stagecoach. A few people walked by and nodded to her, but she didn't see anyone who could be her intended. The stage coach driver took down her two small bags and set them at her feet. He tipped his hat and climbed back on to the coach. The coached creaked and the harnesses jingled as the horses set off in a thunder of hoof beats, leaving a cloud of dust behind.

Standing right across the road from her was a Union Soldier. She instantly shivered. She'd been told the army had left this part of Texas. He stepped down from the wooden walkway, and she turned her back to him. There wasn't a kind word in her body for such a man.

Her heart beat faster as she desperately watched for anyone who could possibly be her intended. Her body relaxed slightly when a wagon was driven between her and the major.

The driver of the wagon was well groomed with rich

caramel colored hair and deep brown eyes. "Miss Nolan?" he asked as he hopped down.

"And you must be Mr. Maxwell," she said with a honeyed southern accent.

He saw the bundle, and his brows furrowed. "Ma'am, is that a baby?"

"Yes, it's my daughter, Bridey." Veronica swallowed hard. He'd be within his rights to send her away. She never mentioned the child. She searched his eyes for understanding, but she didn't find any.

"I see. I thought you said your husband had been dead going on four years now?"

"It's fine Mr. Maxwell. I'll find a job. I didn't tell you because the other ad I answered didn't want my girl. He expected me to give her away. It was a pleasure to correspond with you as well as meet you. Could you point me in the right direction of a rooming house?" She tried to be brave and articulate, but her voice betrayed her and wavered. No one wanted to take on another man's baby.

As she bent to grab both bags in one hand, Bridey began to cry. While she tried to soothe her daughter, one of her bags fell. "Mr. Maxwell, do you know of any other man, a kind man who might take me and Bridey on?"

Maxwell bent down and picked up the bag and then took the other one from her hand. "I think we'll do just fine. There's a wedding planned this afternoon at the ranch if that is all right with you."

Her gaze started at his fine boots up his strong thighs, to his lean waist and to his wide shoulders and strong arms. His lips were twitching when she reached his face.

"Well? Do I pass inspection?"

She widened her eyes. What he must think of her! "You more than meet my expectations Mr. Maxwell." She ducked her heated face and stared at her baby.

"I suspect we should get going," he said. His voice was full of disappointment, but she couldn't blame him.

His hands on her waist as he helped her up sent warmth through her. As soon as she settled herself and Bridey, she shivered. There was something about Mr. Maxwell that affected her. He could have refused her and left her standing on the walk. He hadn't bargained on her child, and she'd been on pins and needles the whole trip from Louisiana.

She couldn't go back—she *wouldn't* go back. She stole a glance at his face and it looked to be set in stone. Oh dear, this didn't bode well.

"Is the ranch far?"

"No, not really."

"I bet it's beautiful!" She smiled hoping he'd turn his head, but he didn't.

He kept driving as though she wasn't there. What had she expected? She was lucky he decided to take her to the ranch. They still weren't married. What if he changed his mind?

Bridey fussed and then cried loudly.

He turned his head. "What's the problem? Is she hungry?" He slowed the wagon to a stop.

"I expect so. I can try to sit in the back and feed her while you drive. She's a very slow eater and she often falls asleep right in the middle. I usually have to stroke her cheek to wake her up to continue."

"Let me set up the blankets so you'll ride more comfortably. It can get a bit bumpy."

Bridey continued to cry as Veronica rocked her and talked to her.

"Here, give me the wee one while you climb in." She hesitated before she handed her baby to him. She scrambled into the back of the wagon and sat on and against the blankets. Bridey wasn't crying.

Mr. Maxwell was smiling and rubbing his nose against

Bridey's. She was wide-eyed and appeared to be fascinated by the big man. He looked up and quickly put Bridey in her arms.

"She's cute as can be." He climbed up onto the wagon and began to drive. He held his back rigid as though he hadn't meant to say Bridey was cute.

Veronica unbuttoned her dress, and Bridey latched on. Just as Veronica expected, the baby fell asleep before she was even moved to the other breast.

"Now, Bridey, you have to put more into your tummy." Veronica stroked her cheek but Bridey still slept.

"Try tickling her feet," Mr. Maxwell suggested.

"That's a fine idea." The tickling of the feet worked, and Bridey woke and latched on again.

"Thank you, Mr. Maxwell. It worked." She didn't expect him to glance at her over his shoulder, and she could feel herself blush from her chest to her forehead when he did. It was a quick glance, but Veronica was a private person. Hopefully, people would respect that about her.

The barn and a big two-story log style house came into view. There were two corrals a bunkhouse, and another good-sized house. Both houses were adorned with gardens containing flowers of various shapes and colors. She had pictured a small ranch with just Mr. Maxwell. Her heart raced. Just how many people lived on the ranch? If Mr. Maxwell told them her husband had died four years ago they would see her shame.

It had been bad enough being a widow and trying to survive. Men thought widows were easy. She'd lost count of how many knocked on her door at night. Then she was with child and the attitude of the community became too much to bear. She refused to name Bridey's father but they all knew who it was. It had been so frightening.

The wagon jolted to a stop and as soon as Mr. Maxwell

was on the ground he came to help her out of the wagon. People seemed to come from every direction to meet them. Her dress was threadbare and she'd mended it numerous times. Her dark hair was dull; somehow it had lost its shine.

She held Bridey close and braced herself for the scandalous names she'd be called. There would be too many questions. Starting over was the worst idea she ever had. She pasted a faint smile on her face and stood next to Mr. Maxwell waiting.

"Oh my," a women with bright blond hair said. "Come, let's get you and the baby inside. You can meet the others later. It must have been an exhausting trip for you."

Veronica stared at the woman and then nodded. She followed her into the house.

"I'm Georgie, come sit down. Would you like some coffee or perhaps water?"

Veronica sat down on a lovely brown sofa. "Coffee doesn't sit well with Bridey."

"Water it is." The gracious women went into another room.

A baby blanket lay across on one of the chairs, and Veronica wondered if there were other children about.

"Here you go." Georgie set the cup on the table in front of the sofa. "Can I take a peek?"

Veronica moved the blanket back from Bridey's head while her stomach churned in dread.

Georgie sat right next to Veronica. "Oh, a girl! How wonderful! How old is she?"

"Four months."

"It must have a long trip for you both. Would you like to rest a bit before the wedding?"

Veronica shook her head. She was too nervous to sleep. "I'm not tired. I'm a bit wound up. You see Mr. Maxwell didn't know I was bringing a baby. I half expect him to call the whole thing off." Her eyes teared, adding to her mortification.

"Babies are always a blessing!"

"May I speak to Mrs. Nolan for a moment?" Mr. Maxwell asked.

Georgie smiled. "Of course, Max. I'll just go check on little Douglas."

Veronica's heart sank but she wasn't surprised. She tried to smile when her intended sat down next to her. To her surprise he took her hand and it had a wonderful calming effect.

"May I call you Veronica? I go by Max instead of Austin. "

She nodded not trusting her voice.

"Your husband died four years ago?"

"Yes," she hung her head.

"You've had a hard time of it, haven't you? So many of our loved ones never came home from the war. Those that did aren't the same. I heard it's been bad in Louisiana with the riots and the killings. I would be proud to have you as my wife. The other house you saw as we drove up is to be ours." A grin spread across his face. "We built it in record time. The reverend will be here in a less than an hour." He leaned forward and caught an errant tear on Veronica's cheek with his thumb.

"Yes, I'll be ready." She glanced up at him and expected a smile, but she had the strange feeling that Max was marrying her because he was a man who kept his word. Without saying anything else, he left the house.

A tall, dark man walked in. "I'm Parker, Georgie's husband. I have strict orders to pour the hot water for your bath and then to guard against any male from coming near the house." He smiled. "Max is lucky to have you. He's been looking forward to this day."

"I've been looking forward to it too." She watched as he

filled the copper tub with water. "A towel is on the chair and so is the soap. Knowing Georgie she'll be down to help you. She's so excited to have another woman on the ranch." He finished and was about to go out the door when a woman came in. "This is Sondra. She helps Georgie around the house."

Sondra wasn't much older than Veronica. She wore her hair in one long braid down her back. It was brown and shiny. "Let's get you into the tub and ready for your wedding. I'm so excited, and I'm not the one getting married."

Sondra turned her back and Veronica undressed and got into the tub. As she slipped her body under the steamy water she sighed. She took the soap, and it smelled like lavender.

"Here, I'll wash your hair," Sondra offered.

"I'll get your dress pressed. Which bag is it in?" Georgie asked.

"I thought the dress I was wearing would be fitting. I haven't seen new fabric in years."

"We've all been there. I have one I think will work." Georgie went back up the stairs.

"She's a nice woman," Veronica said.

"She sure is. She had a hard time of it too, only in Tennessee. She knows how you feel." Sondra finished rinsing Veronica's hair.

Her bags had been set on the floor in the sitting room. She wrapped herself in a towel and took out clean underthings to wear. They too were threadbare. There was no help for it. She put them on.

Georgie brought down a pretty blue dress with white trim. It was so beautiful that it brought tears to Veronica's eyes.

"No tears, it's your wedding day. We have to hurry," she said as she helped Veronica into the dress. "There, you look beautiful."

Sondra nodded. "You sure do. I'm staying inside to watch the little ones. You two best get there."

Sondra gave Veronica's hand a quick squeeze before Georgie led her out to the porch. Too many people were there to watch her, to judge her, to find her lacking. For a moment, she felt dizzy. She got a hold of herself and set her shoulders and raised her chin as her mother had taught her.

A bouquet of flowers rested on the porch rail, and Georgie picked it up and handed it to Veronica. "A perfect bride!" Let's go."

Georgie went down the aisle between all the people standing. She smiled at them and Veronica wished she felt as happy. It felt less like an aisle and more like a plank. She swallowed hard and while keeping her gaze on Max she walked to him.

Max recognized the dress Veronica wore, and it looked nice on her. Her long brown hair hung around her shoulders and down her back. She seemed of fine disposition. There was no indication she was shrew. She'd lived on a farm, so she must be used to cooking and the like. But the baby was part of the bargain and the omission of Bridey in the letters bothered him He had a good heart but could he learn to love the baby obviously born on the wrong side of the blanket?

He wasn't sure if it changed his opinion of Veronica or not. Maybe once she told him how Bridey came about he'd feel differently. A baby was innocent, but the parents weren't. There was something he didn't know, and he had a feeling he didn't want to know. A sense of satisfaction came over him. At least he'd won the house.

He smiled thinking about how Sandler brought home the oldest saloon girl Max had ever seen. She didn't even have more than three teeth. Georgie's face had been full of horror. She wanted weddings and babies not grandmothers.

The Reverend started the wedding.

Max's mind drifted off again. Poor Willis had almost got himself full of buckshot. He'd climbed into the window of a sweet young girl with the intent of proposing, but her father hadn't seen it that way. The next day, her father had come to talk to Parker about his purity-robbing men.

The reverend asked him if he would take Veronica for his wife.

"I do," he said in response and then he fished the ring out of his pocket. He'd carried it with him for years. It had been his mother's. He slid the gold ring inlaid with emeralds onto Veronica's finger, and tears filled her eyes. He smiled at her, and his heart felt full as he leaned down and kissed her. He had to admit that the kiss was a bit of a disappointment. She was very quick to pull away.

"The ring is beautiful, Max. Thank you."

"It was my mother's. It's brought me luck all these years. It looks good on you." He could have sworn her eyes glowed for an instant.

Taking her hand in his, he introduced her to the men. A few wanted to give her a kiss, but he quickly put an end to that notion. Poor Whitley ended up with a bloodied nose, and that dissuaded anyone else from touching her.

Sandler shook his hand. "You did it. You won the house. I thought for sure it would be me."

Max felt his bride stiffen beside him. That remark was bound to cause trouble. "It's a fine house."

Willis joined them, shaking his head. "I put a lot of work into that house thinking I'd be the one who'd win the bet. Almost had it too, if her father hadn't had a gun." He grinned. "Best wishes to you both."

Max gave Veronica a sidelong glance. She was looking in

a different direction, away from him and his friends. He'd have a lot of explaining to do.

"I'm going to check on Bridey." She turned and began to walk away.

"What's with her having a baby? Didn't her husband die in the war?" Sandler asked rather loudly.

Veronica stopped for a second then she continued on to the house. She must have heard.

"I don't know much about the baby, and I wasn't going to ask. Not yet, anyway. I'd appreciate it if you didn't mention the bet or the baby. It upset Veronica. No one wants to know they are part of a bet or a contest."

Willis and Sandler both made noises he took as agreement. Max had always lived a life of integrity. He made sure there wasn't a thing others could say about him except that he was a good soldier. He sighed as he rubbed the back of his neck. He'd have to make a show of accepting both his wife and her child. Why he'd thought it would all be easy, he didn't know.

Parker slapped him on the back. "You all right?"

"A few unexpected surprises is all. Nothing I can't handle."

Parker cocked his right brow. "You have a ready-made family, and I know you didn't count on the baby. If you need someone to talk to, I'm always here."

"Why didn't she just tell me? It wouldn't have made a difference." His smile felt as hollow as his heart. "I appreciate your offer. I'll probably take you up on it."

Veronica walked out of the house with Bridey in her arms. She glanced around and then smiled when she saw him.

"She sure is pretty." Parker slapped him on the back again. "Go and stand by your wife. Your reaction to the child will matter how she is treated by the rest."

Max slowly walked to his family. She really was beautiful, though her eyes looked haunted and she could use a few pounds. Who knew what she had endured in Louisiana? Had anyone been there for her, to protect her?

She gave him a smile of delight as he approached. He grinned back and held his hands out. He hugged Bridey to him then he held her so they were eye to eye. "I'm your pa. You are a bonnie one, aren't you? I expect we'll get on just fine." He held Bridey in one arm as he held Veronica's hand in his. He still had many questions but he was determined to have a nice day and make sure both his girls were accepted in the community.

He introduced them to Willian Cabot, the foreman, to Walter Green, a fellow soldier and Sondra's beau, Anson Stack, owner of the general store, Daniel Willford, the town banker, and to Shelly Kingsman, restaurant owner. Next, he introduced her to neighboring ranchers, Jamie Butcher, Zach McBride, and Dace McKenna. Everyone was polite, and they seemed to like her.

He wanted to growl as a gaggle of women came over to them. They were young women who still acted like immature southern belles. "Hello Fanny, Constance, and Henrietta. This is Veronica, my wife and Bridey, my daughter."

He watched in disdain as they acted shocked and dismayed that Veronica had a child.

"Recently widowed, you poor dear," Fanny commented with a bit of malice in her voice. Being the town gossips they already knew the whole story.

"Isn't that Georgie's dress? You didn't bring your own?" Constance asked cattily.

"I don't suppose we'll see much of each other," Henrietta said. "We can't risk our reputations." She gave his wife a superior smile.

They all turned at once and walked away. Veronica flinched and lowered her head.

"Veronica?" he said softly. "Honey, don't let them get you down. Henrietta tried to get me to court her, and I gave her set down that I guess she'll never forgot. Honestly, Georgie doesn't talk to them. They tried to shame her about her clothes, but when she told them she was an O'Rourke they realized they'd insulted the most powerful family in the south."

The rest of the cowhands came and paid their respects, and although Veronica smiled, there was a sadness about her.

"Let's get you off your feet for a bit." He led her to bench under a willow tree. "Here take Bridey and I'll get us something to drink."

She nodded and took Bridey, but her eyes shimmered and he was afraid she would start crying. He hurried and got the punch and then asked Georgie to talk to Veronica. Veronica wiped away a tear and tried to smile when they approached.

Georgie sat next to her and took Bridey. "There are people like the belles no matter where you go. They've insulted me many times. But if you notice we're married and live on this beautiful ranch. They don't even have beaus. They are mean and spiteful and they weren't invited. Don't take what they had to say to heart. When I first got here all I had was rags to wear. That was just the way it was for most southerners. We are survivors and the only thing that upset them about the war was the fact there weren't any parties."

"I shouldn't be so sensitive. It's been a long day"

Georgie tilted her head. "If you'd two would like to go rest at your new house, go ahead. I can keep Bridey with me for a bit."

Veronica looked at Max. He nodded and she smiled a real smile. "Thank you. I will take Bridey with us though. I won't rest if she's not near me."

Georgie handed the baby back to her, and then Max took Veronica's hand and helped her up from the bench. He entwined his fingers with hers and walked her to their new home.

HER NERVES HIT her all at once, and she tried to pretend to be as calm as possible. "It's a lovely house."

"We finished last week, and Georgie bought a few pieces of furniture. She said the woman who ended up living here would like to pick things out for herself." He drew her up onto the porch, opened the door, and then swept both her and Bridey up into his arms. He carried them into the house.

Her heart beat faster. His actions touched her, and a rush of pleasure washed over her. She actually laughed. It sounded foreign to her. It'd been so long since a carefree laugh had come out of her mouth.

Max put her down on her feet. "Let me show you the bedroom."

She closed her eyes for a moment. It was her wedding night or rather late afternoon. She'd been preparing herself mentally for it. "Of course."

"Your bags were brought here already." He opened a door to a spacious room with an awfully big bed. There was also a chair, a side table, and a wardrobe.

"Oh my, it's lovely. I've never seen a bed so big, and I'm used to pegs on the wall to hang my clothes on." She walked to the bed, admiring the quilt. It was a well-known wedding quilt pattern. Max was too good for her. She'd always lived in very small farmhouses until things took a turn and then she'd lived in shacks. Her shoulders slumped. She'd never live up to his idea of a wife. She had too many secrets she planned to carry to her grave.

"Max, this house is too grand for me. I shouldn't have put this fine dress on. I'm not a fine lady like Georgie. My folks were always poor. You're a fine man, and you deserve a fine lady." She sat on the bed and tried her best not to cry.

"Are you wanted by the law?"

"No, of course not."

"Did you work in a brothel?"

Her eyes widened. "No, didn't you read my letter? I might have been poor and a woman alone but I never— The answer is no."

"Is your husband really dead?"

"Yes."

Max sat on the bed next to her. "You are good enough for me. It's easy to doubt yourself when you're in a new place. So far, I like you. I think we'll get on just fine. From what I've observed, marriage is giving and taking. But you've been married before, so you know."

"I'm just tired I guess."

"Listen, take a nap and get some rest. It looks as though the baby is finally asleep."

She gazed into his eyes looking for disappointment. Seeing none, she nodded. "It sounds like a good idea."

He stood and kissed her on the forehead. "Get some sleep. I'll be here if you need me."

"Thank you, Max."

He closed the door behind him as he left.

Veronica stood and placed Bridey on the bed. "I know your ma would have approved of Max and now we're out of danger, little one." She lay down next to the baby and fell asleep.

CHAPTER THREE

*V*eronica woke with a start to Bridey's cry. After changing the baby, Veronica unbuttoned her dress and held the little one close. The door opened, and Max walked in. His face turned a nice shade of cherry red.

"I'm sorry."

"Don't be. I'll be feeding her a lot, so you might as well get used to it. It's part of being a parent. I'm just glad that I'm able to give her sustenance. Many women had a hard time. I think it was due to worry and fear. This is the most relaxed I've been in about a year."

Max looked everywhere except at her. She bit back a smile. He'd get used to it.

"I was embarrassed at first too. But this is natural to me now. I was thinking that we could line a drawer with a quilt and Bridey could sleep there."

His brows furrowed.

"Just until we get her a cradle. I didn't have one for her so I used a drawer. I've learned to make do. I'll need to wash the diapers too."

"Today?"

"Yes. I just used her last clean one. It hasn't been easy keeping her clean all the way here."

Max gazed at her finally. "I suppose hot water is in order?"

"That would be perfect." He seemed so easy going. It was a huge weight off her shoulders.

"I'll get the cook stove working and water on to boil, then I'll get some lye soap from Georgie."

She grimaced. "I don't want to bother Georgie."

Max chuckled. "She'd be insulted if she found out we didn't ask."

Gazing into his blue eyes, she felt as though she was getting lost in them. He was surprisingly handsome. He could have had any woman, but he decided on a mail order bride. It seemed a bit strange.

He left the room, and she could hear him lighting the cook stove and putting water on to boil. She wasn't used to a cook stove. But she was a good cook, and she'd just have to figure it out. As soon as he went outside again, she put Bridey down and took off Georgie's dress. She shouldn't have slept in it, but at least it didn't look wrinkled.

Next, she opened one of her bags and pulled out a brown dress. It, too, had seen better days. It had been let out and then taken in and taken in again. All of her dresses were dark in color since stains didn't show as badly. Making do was something she was an expert on. Now, to be sure she didn't shame her husband with her backward ways. She could read and write but figuring had always been hard for her.

Bridey was asleep again, so Veronica grabbed the diapers and put them in a pail of cold water to soak for a bit. The temptation to fiddle with the stove was hard to fight but she didn't want to take a chance of letting the fire die. Max could teach her.

The kitchen was large with a nice table for eating. Was

that a water pump? There were cabinets with doors on them. She'd never seen anything like it. She opened and closed all of them. Then she peeked into the other bedroom and it was nice and big too. It was empty but it was a room for dreamin' about future children. Next she went out to the main room. The fireplace took up a large portion of one wall. She'd be warm this winter.

There were a few shelves and her smile grew extra wide. There were plenty of books to read. Ignorant people didn't read, and she wasn't ignorant. The house got plenty of light. She touched one of the windows and was awed by the glass panes. There were shutters too. The wooden floor was covered with a very big rug.

She didn't belong here. Her family had a farm but had to become sharecroppers after the civil war. Even at their best they never had the likes of things in this house. Max probably thought he married a normal woman down on her luck, not a woman who was out of luck and never really had any.

Her heart beat quickly, and perspiration formed on her brow. What had she done? She wouldn't be an asset to her husband. She was bound to shame him, and she knew there would be plenty of questions about Bridey. She shouldn't have come. It was all a big mistake.

The door opened, and Max came in with the soap. He smiled at her.

If she told him he'd send her home. Drawing in a deep breath, she let it out slowly and followed him into the kitchen. He put soap in the water, and she put the diapers into the boiling water.

"Could you show me how to use the hand pump?" She waited for his dismay that she didn't know how, but his expression didn't change.

"Here, you just lift the handle up and then down, water

comes out. You put the pail or cup under it. The sink has a stopper to collect the water to do dishes."

"How do you empty the water?"

He smiled. "This is the best part. You pull out the stopper and the water runs out."

She furrowed her brow. "Runs out to where?"

"There is a pipe that draws it away a bit."

Her jaw dropped. "It just magically leaves the house? Oh my." She sighed. "You must think me inept, but we never had luxuries in my home. This house is amazing. It has glass window panes, and did you see the rug?"

She liked his smile. He looked to be enjoying himself.

"I do have something to confess. I can cook using the fireplace, but I'm not sure what to do with a cook stove." She watched him intently, waiting for a frown.

"I'll show you. We'll make supper together, and then I'll show you how to bank it for tomorrow. Do you see the compartment in back? It's a water reserve. You fill it with water and you'll always have warm water. Not hot enough to wash diapers, but it'll make you smile when you wash your face in the mornings. No more cold water." He put his arms around her and pulled her to him. "You'll like it here."

She tried not to panic. She didn't like being close to men. Arms encircling her made her feel trapped. She drew away slowly and relaxed a bit when he let her go. It was just another thing he wouldn't like about her. Pretending was harder than she'd imagined.

"I'm a hard worker, and as soon as I know how it all works you won't have to lift a finger around here."

"Sit down, I want to talk to you," Max said.

Her stomach clenched as she sat at the table across from him.

"What type of man was your husband?"

"He was a good man."

Max rubbed the back of his neck. "I guess I want to know if he was gentle with you or if he got mad when things weren't done."

She had no idea. She never lived with him. "He was a nice man. It was my father who demanded everything be done. I guess I lived in fear of him, and I don't want to do anything to make you want to hit me."

Anger crossed his face. "I don't believe in hitting or manhandling women. If we have a problem I hope we can talk it out."

Her shoulders relaxed. "I'll finish up with the wash." She got up and kept her back to him. What was he going to think tonight when she shied away from him? She'd have to get through it somehow.

MAX WALKED to the main house, his fists clenched tight. Something was wrong, and he couldn't think of what he'd done. He'd pretended that her bringing her surprise baby didn't bother him. He'd been more than kind, or so he thought. He'd been a soldier too long, and he had no idea what to do with a wife.

Parker and Georgie stood up when he reached the porch. "I need to talk to both of you." He let himself into the house. He paced back and forth while the couple sat down on the sofa.

"Are Veronica and the baby all right?" Georgie asked.

He ran his hand over his face and then shook his head. "I don't know. I mean they're fine but something is going on. I've never spent much time in the company of women, but she seems so nervous."

"It's probably natural," Parker advised.

"I was nervous coming to Texas, and my clothes were in

the same condition if you remember." Georgie stood. "I'll get us some punch, and I'll fill a basket of food for your dinner."

Max stopped pacing. "That would be a big help, thank you." He watched as Georgie and Parker exchanged worried glances.

"Is it the baby? Did she say who the father is?"

"Not a word, and I'm sure I'll get used to the girl. I just wasn't expecting a child. I don't think Veronica likes me. She flinches when I get near her. I've tried being kind and helpful, but I'm at a loss as to how to act around her." He sighed and sagged into a chair.

"She flinched when I congratulated her, so I don't think it's you. I would have thought the country would have settled by now but in some parts of the south there is still a lot of violence. Maybe something happened. You're right to be put off by her omission of Bridey. I guess she was desperate. I'm sure she'll tell you. She's probably worried about the wedding night. You two really don't know each other."

"She did mention that her pa used to hit her. Maybe that's why she cringes when I get too close. She did want to know if I was a hitting type of man." He drew his brows together, considering what he could do for a moment then sighed. "I guess I'll let her alone until we know each other. I don't want her to be afraid. I mean she was married and all."

Parker put both hands on his knees. "I think the answer lies with how she got with child. Sometimes you have to wait until a woman decides she wants to tell you."

Max shook his head. He didn't know much more than when he'd walked over. He stood and Georgie magically appeared. He gave her a knowing look, and she blushed.

"Parker is right. She seems really nice, Max. Patience is the key." She handed him the basket and herded him out the door before he could thank her. He never did get any punch.

Did he have enough patience? He always liked to act on

something rather than wait. But he'd been patient when he had to be.

He walked into the house and put the basket on the table. Then he peered into the bedroom and quickly turned around. "I'm sorry. I didn't even think, I guess I'm not used to having a wife yet."

"Max this is your home. You have no reason to be sorry. Since I seem to have to feed her a lot, I'd say you'll get used to it rather quickly. When I'm done you can teach me how to work that stove."

He turned back toward her but didn't look at her. "Georgie sent me home with a big basket of food. I doubt we'll need to cook tonight."

"You could show me how to make coffee?"

He chuckled. "You're anxious to learn. Most people would avoid it if they could."

"If I don't learn the basics tonight, there will be no breakfast tomorrow," she said softly.

He gazed at her. She was more beautiful than he'd imagined. "Coffee tonight and I'll help you tomorrow."

"My initial impression of you was right. You're a sweet man. Not many men would help a woman. I appreciate it." Her smile was as close to being angelic as a smile could get. He thought he felt a longing for her, but that was impossible. He hardly knew her.

"She fell asleep."

"Your suggestion of tickling her feet works the best."

He watched as Veronica lightly stroked the baby's feet. Bridey woke with a little smile and allowed her mother to switch her to the other breast. His face heated, and he stopped staring. "I'll set out the food."

She certainly was a puzzle. He would have thought she'd hate for him to see her feeding Bridey, but she was fine with it. He'd ride into town tomorrow and get her and the baby some clothes.

Now, how to approach the question of the wedding night?

———

"Bridey I think we'll have a good life here. Max seems nice, and the ranch is so pretty. Maybe I'll learn to ride a horse." Bridey gurgled at her.

Veronica watched Max pour the coffee. One of her greatest fears had been getting a husband that was cruel.

"What's that smile for?" Max said in a teasing voice.

"It's for you. I never expected someone kind, and I certainly didn't expect a new house. No more leaking roof and the door actually closes. I just hope I don't wake up and find it all to be a dream."

He pulled out a chair for her to sit on. "She sure is a bonnie baby."

"Yes, thank you."

"Would you like anything in your coffee?"

"I don't think anyone ever asked me before, but no, I drink it black. I'm just glad you have coffee. We ran out and... well, we ran out." She'd gotten slapped good for running out too.

He watched her, and she grew uncomfortably warm. She sipped her coffee pretending she didn't notice his regard, but grew more and more nervous as the sun began to go down.

"I've thought about our wedding night," he suddenly announced, "and I hope you agree that we should wait until you feel more comfortable here with me." He reached across the table and gave her hand a pat before he pulled his hand back.

"If you keep being so gentlemanly you'll make me cry. It's

been a long hard road ever since the war started, and even though it's been over, many act as though it's still going on. Thank you, I would like to get to know you better. I've been so nervous about tonight. I can make a pallet in the other bedroom."

"I think that bed is plenty big enough for us to share without us noticing the other is even there. We'll have Bridey in the room as well. I'm a man of my word." He was staring again.

There was nothing to do but accept his offer. "You're right, I've never seen such a big bed, and we'll make a nice soft spot for Bridey in an empty drawer. I'd hate to have someone roll over on her."

His lips twitched. "I can see you're assuming that someone would be me."

She widened her eyes hoping she hadn't offended him, but then he chuckled and she calmed.

"I don't know if you're a roller or not. I do have to warn ya though. I have nightmares once in a while." She stared at her coffee.

"It's nothing to be embarrassed about. Most of us have nightmares now and then. I think many of us saw or experienced things no one should have. It's fine, and if you need me I'll be right there."

They ate with very little conversation, and then she stood. "I'll put Bridey down and then clean up the kitchen. I'll be right back."

Once in the bedroom, she fixed a drawer for Bridey, who was happy to lie in it. Looking at the bed, it suddenly seemed smaller than before. Perhaps it was the idea of sharing it that made it more likely that they'd end up touching at some point. What if she shot out of bed and ended up running outside? She'd be sure to stiffen if he even brushed against her.

He'd have many questions she'd have to answer sooner than later, and it made her stomach churn. He'd have her on the next stagecoach back home. Taking a breath, she turned and left the room. It wasn't fair to saddle him with her problems, not that she had anywhere to go. She'd expected anything but kindness and she thanked God for her good fortune.

She should have known. The kitchen was already clean.

"Ready to learn about the stove?" His smile was infectious and she smiled right back at him.

<hr>

HE STOOD outside the bedroom door wondering if he should knock on it. He figured he'd given Veronica long enough to get changed and into bed. It would be much easier if he wasn't so attracted to her. The alternating pain and happiness in her blue eyes could be felt in his heart. Her walnut brown hair might be unbound. He liked the way it had swirled down her back at the wedding.

Sighing, he bowed his head. He needed a clear mind. He'd think of anything but her. War maneuvers might be the thing to keep his mind occupied. He lightly knocked and opened the door. She was sitting up in bed with the sheet up around her neck. She looked as though she was going to the gallows.

"I'm going to get undressed if you wanted to turn your head." He undressed while she turned away. He left his drawers on. "No peeking now," he teased. Before she could react he slid under the sheet being careful not to touch her.

Her hair was braided, and it hung down the side of her head to the front of her. It was as thick as his wrist and long. He practically gulped. He reached to the little table on his side of the bed and lowered the lamp.

"You'll need to see to feed Bridey?"

28

"Yes, thank you. Good night."

"Good night." *War maneuvers, war maneuvers, a soldier should always...Who was he fooling?* He was a healthy man and wondering what she looked like under her nightgown—which he had yet to see—was perfectly normal. Wasn't it?

It wasn't the most restful night. She fed Bridey and it took a long while to get her back to sleep. Then, after all was quiet she cried out and sat straight up. He turned over and saw the terror in her eyes.

"It was just a dream. You're safe here with me." Should he try to comfort her? He decided not to chance it but it was hard not to. She looked lost and so very young.

"Can I get you a glass of water?"

She slid back down into the bed and turned so her back faced him. "No, thank you. I'm fine."

From the way her voice wavered there was no way she was fine, but he'd let her be. It was hard to sleep as she tossed and turned, but he didn't make a sound. So, this was marriage.

CHAPTER FOUR

"*D*o you need anything from town?" Max asked. He took another bite of the eggs they'd made together. If it wasn't sad, he would have thought it comical, the way she tried to be near enough to learn but far enough away to keep her distance. Her face hadn't turned back to the lovely rosy color it had become when she woke up with her head on his chest.

"No, I have everything I need." Her reply sounded matter of fact, but he knew better.

"What about the baby? Surely she could use something?"

Her eyes gleamed for a moment then she shook her head. "We're fine."

"I'll be getting along now. Spring Water is the closest town. I'll be back later this afternoon. I have to go to the blacksmith's smithy to see if he has shovels and hoes for gardening. I have no idea how Parker's mother got her vegetables planted, but we need some. I'll stop over and get Georgie's list too." He finished the last of his coffee and stood. He put his hat on. "Why don't you try to relax today?"

He hesitated. Normally a husband would give his wife a kiss before leaving, wouldn't he?

"Be safe," she said rather stiffly.

"I will." He left the house and went to see Georgie. She'd know what a baby needed. He had a good idea what to buy Veronica since he'd done the same for Georgie when she first arrived.

Sondra opened the door when he knocked. She smiled brightly at him. "I hope ya enjoyed your wedding night." She stepped aside so he could enter.

"Max!" Georgie greeted. "Well, how did it go?"

His gaze went from one woman to the other as his face heated. "I think it's a private matter between me and my wife."

He wanted to laugh when both women frowned. "I'm going to town—"

"Oh good, I'll grab the list," Sondra said as she hurried to the kitchen.

"Georgie, I know what to get for a woman but not for a baby."

"You've come to the right place. Buy the softest white fabric you can find and lots of it. Get enough for underthings for Veronica and baby gowns. Ask Anson at the general store about material for diapers, sewing items and maybe a ragdoll. I know she's too young but I think Veronica would take it as a sign that you like Bridey. Some pretty material for dresses and then go to the dress shop. Nancy Mathers has ready-made dresses. Get a couple of those and a soft night-gown. Oh dear, I didn't look at her shoes."

"I did. I made a tracing of the boots she wore. I'll see if they have any in her size. Now what about a few ribbons? I know women like them."

"I think she'll like anything you get for her." A sad smile appeared on Georgie's face. "I don't think she's had anything nice in her whole life. It's time for you to change that for her. I'll stop by in a while to visit with her."

Sondra hurried back and handed him a list. "You might want to get some food for your house. There's some we put there before you moved in, but you'll need more."

Max took the list and watched Sondra hurry back to the kitchen. He bent and kissed Georgie on the cheek. "You've been a big help. Thank you."

As he went down the porch steps, he heard Parker ask Georgie about the kiss. Hopefully his marriage would be as happy as theirs.

THE UNION OFFICERS continued to make sure no one brought a gun into town. They liked to be sure that everyone knew they were still the law in these parts. Max ignored them mostly. He drove the wagon to the checkpoint. Sergeant Hollanda was there, and Max wanted to groan. There was bad blood between his men and Parker's men.

"Maxwell. Kill anyone today?" Hollanda asked sarcastically.

He forced himself to keep a blank face. "Not yet."

Hollanda nodded. "Keep it that way. Let him by."

Max drove the wagon to the general store and reined the horses to a stop. He put on the brake and then hopped down.

He walked into the store and was surprised to see it busy. He greeted those he walked by to get to the back counter. "Morning Anson. When you get time could you double the order that's on the list? I also need to buy fabric and some other things. Why is it so busy in here?"

"People are buying supplies and ammo. There was an incident with those white hoods last night. One of the women was killed and not in a very nice way. They have everyone upended waiting to see who is next."

33

"Bad business, and a shame. Did the Union Army do anything about it?"

Anson frowned and shrugged one shoulder. "They don't think it's a problem. Now tell me if I'm wrong but I thought they fought us confederates so the slaves could be free. Now that they are free they have no interest in protecting them." He lowered his voice. "I really shouldn't be talking about it. You never know who is behind those hoods."

"You're right about that. I'm supposed to ask about material for diapers."

Anson smiled. "Oh, for the little one. I have it marked with a sign. It's one of the most asked questions."

"I have a few places to stop by before I come back, so no hurry." He turned around and noticed that people were eyeing him and whispering. What the devil? He scowled at them and kept walking right out to the wooden walkway.

His spurs jangled against the wood as he walked to the dress shop. Parker had financed the shop so carpetbaggers wouldn't get ahold of it as they had with a lot of the other businesses.

He went inside and was glad he was the only customer. "Miss Mathers," he greeted as he tipped his hat.

She smiled brightly. "I had a feeling you'd be here. I gathered a few things together I think should fit your new wife. You're a lucky man, Maxwell."

"That I am." He admired her cheerful disposition, and she had the prettiest blond hair. He would have asked her to marry him, but her heart still belonged to her beau who had been killed in the war.

"Let me show you what I have and you can pick a few if you like." She went into the back and returned with several garments. "I picked mostly practical dresses for a ranch plus one for church or any other special occasion. I'm adding a nightgown as my wedding gift."

She showed them to him one by one, and he picked all but the brown and charcoal colored dresses. Four new practical dresses, one frilly dusty rose colored one and a nightgown. That should hold her until she had time sew more. How many dresses did a woman need? "Do you have a shawl for church?"

"Of course I do. I'll wrap them all up. Where is your wagon?"

"At the general store." He paused and glanced around. "Do you know why people were whispering about me?"

She looked away for a moment. "It's the baby. When she accepted your proposal you told everyone her husband had died a few years ago. It'll die down."

He paid the bill and left. He'd been able to rein his temper in until he was out of the store. Who did these people think they were? He went to the smithy and got his garden tools and heard more about the men with hoods. Then he walked back to the general store.

Thankfully, most of the other customers had gone. He'd calmed himself as much as he could while he looked at fabric. Constance McPherson, one of the belles, sidled up next to him.

She opened her mouth and drew a breath.

He gave her the nastiest look he could muster. "Don't say a word."

Her eyes widened, and she stepped away from him and then hurried from the store.

Anson came and helped him pick out material for Veronica and Bridey. He even showed Max where the dolls were. "I probably cost you a sale."

"Not at all. I was glad to see her leave. Anything else?"

"Yes, I'd like some ribbon and some lace for the dresses. Oh, and some of those pretty buttons."

Anson got Max's order filled and helped him put it all

into his wagon. "Just you remember you're the one who has someone to love. Judgment and gossip is not right, especially in hard times like these. I think you're one lucky man." He shook Max's hand.

"Thank you."

"Oh, here comes Nancy. Now if only I could be that blessed." Anson sighed.

Max thanked them both as he finished loading up. Driving away, he caught sight of them talking together and smiled. Thankfully, the sergeant wasn't at the checkpoint, so he was waved right on.

As he drove, he thought about the gossip, and by the time he returned to the ranch he didn't like it but he decided he couldn't really blame people. He'd had his questions and doubts too.

He pulled up in front of his house and asked Willis to help him unload the wagon and then take the rest over to Georgie. Veronica's eyes were so wide he thought maybe he had gone overboard with his purchases.

SHE'D NEVER SEEN SO many packages in her life, and that didn't include the bountiful items of food. "Surely these can't all be for me?"

His eyes danced as he grinned. "Yes, you needed a few things."

"A few? Oh my. May I open one?" She bit her lip waiting for a response.

"Of course! In fact, open them all."

They were all wrapped up in brown paper and string. She took the string off one package and pulled back the paper and gasped. A dress! A ready-made dress. Reaching out she touched the blue fabric. She pulled it out and looked at it, and she couldn't contain her delight. "It looks like it'll be a great fit!"

"Nancy Mathers owns a dress shop. She saw you at the wedding and guessed at your size. She usually has dresses already made in her shop. Go on, there are more to open." He seemed to enjoy watching her open the packages.

She opened a few more dresses, each more lovely than the rest. And then she opened one and wanted to cry. It was a light rose-colored dress. "I've never seen anything so lovely in my entire life. This is not for the likes of me. I'd feel as though I'm putting on airs." She touched the ruffles and the lace. She wanted the dress but it wouldn't be practical.

"You could wear it to church or any gatherings." He spoke quietly, with a hopeful tone. "I think it would look nice on you."

"To church…" She felt as though her body glowed. Impulsively, she hugged Max. "Thank you." She quickly put distance between them.

The nightgown was the softest she'd ever felt. Then she opened a package with fabric, yards and yards of material for making clothing, and most of it was cheerful calico in assorted colors. The buttons, lace, and ribbons brought tears to her eyes. She stopped when Bridey began to fuss.

To her surprise, Max picked the baby up and rocked her in his big strong arms. Something inside of her opened, and she felt so much emotion watching him.

"Open that one at the edge of the table."

She looked to where he pointed and opened the package. Tears streamed down her face as she held the small doll. She smiled through her tears and brought the doll to Bridey. It was almost as big as she was but Bridey cooed at it.

"You sweet, sweet man. No one has ever given anything to her before. I often wondered what would become of her."

Max flushed, and Veronica warmed inside.

"The last two are diaper material and soft white cloth for underthings and baby gowns."

"I don't know how I'll ever be able to thank you. Next time buy some yard goods so I can make you some new clothing. Would you mind holding her while I put this blue dress on?"

He chuckled. "No, you go ahead."

As soon as she closed the bedroom door tears poured down her face. Not a single person had been so good to her before. Everything was amazing, but the doll for Bridey touched her so deeply. She needed to tell him the truth, but how? When?

She washed her face and put the dress on. On a whim, she let her hair down and shyly left the bedroom. Max looked up at her and stared. "Is something wrong?"

He shook his head. "You're beautiful. Your hair is glorious."

She felt her face heat and gazed at the floor. It wasn't true, but it was nice of him to say.

A knock on the door drew her attention, and she answered it. Parker gave her a quick smile. "I need to speak to Max. It's important."

Max handed Bridey to Veronica and walked out the door with Parker. It looked serious.

She got Bridey settled in her drawer and set about putting her treasures away. Imagine all this for one person. What would she do with the new dresses and ones she made? And lace? Her heart filled with gratefulness. After quickly putting her hair up, she changed back into her old dress and vowed that the first thing she sewed would be an apron.

She heard loud voices and looked out the front window. A group of men had gathered; many whom she recognized. It appeared to be trouble, and she'd hoped to have left trouble behind in Louisiana.

She listened to the men argue. It wasn't eavesdropping since they were loud enough for anyone to hear.

Parker held his hand up signaling for silence. "We need to protect those who can't protect themselves. The blasted Union Army refuses to get involved. If the North really wanted to help, they'd have found jobs and places for the former slaves to live. There are so many displaced soldiers and now the slaves. The South isn't what it was and it's up to men like us to help rebuild it without violence. I'm going to hire some of the freedmen to help with the ranch. If anyone has a problem working alongside them, please just leave. No judgment. I will not tolerate any type of bullying. We'll also need to provide living quarters. I'd welcome suggestions. Many have families with nowhere to go. I'm going to ride out tomorrow and talk with a few of the leaders and see what they'd think would be a good plan."

His words were met with shuffling feet and murmurs, but he held up his hand for silence.

"I fully expect to be spit upon by some of the townspeople, and we'll have to be extra diligent about guard duty. A woman was pulled out of her house last night, abused and tortured then hanged. Her crime? She asked around for a job." He swung his gaze over the crowd. "The old ways are gone, and we need to make Texas safe for all people. We have two babies on the ranch right now, and I'd hate to think of the future for them if we don't step in. I won't lie, it's going to be dangerous. If you go to town, go in pairs or don't go. You won't have your guns on you and since the men who killed that woman wore hoods over their heads, we don't know who the enemy is."

The murmur swelled again, a little louder this time, but once again, Parker brought the men under control with a sweep of his hand.

"Just so there aren't any hard feelings, if you do decide to light out, you can take the horse you usually ride. That's all. Give it some thought, and we'll meet again after supper." Parker turned and walked to his house.

Chills spread through her body. Perhaps she should have gone north. She couldn't seem to stop shaking. She was here now, so she'd have to make sure the house had enough rifles in it to ward off whatever may come. Fear haunted her as she put her gifts from Max away. She wondered if any of the ranch men rode with the white hoods. That's what caused more fear than anything. They could be anyone. A neighbor, a shopkeeper, a friend's husband. There was just no way to know. Too many people harbored hate in their hearts.

Bridey fussed, and Veronica lifted her into her arms. At one time, she'd thought she wouldn't be able to be a good mother to Bridey, but she loved her with all her heart. Children were innocents, and they shouldn't have to carry the burden of their birth with them their whole lives.

The door opened and Max walked in looking rather worried. His hat was off and it looked as though he'd run his fingers through his hair more than a few times. It stuck on end in places.

"How many rifles are in the house?"

Max scowled at her question. "Why?"

"If there is trouble coming, I'm defending myself. I'll not be caught unaware again."

His shoulders sagged. "You heard."

"Yes, I did, and this type of thing is just starting. It's bound to get worse. That's why I left my home and came here. I know you can protect us, but you're not always here and I'm a good shot."

"We're having a meeting after supper. I'll grab a few rifles and pistols for the house. I don't want you to feel scared." He opened his arms and she gladly walked into them with

Bridey in her arms. He made her feel safe, and she sighed as she snuggled closer to him.

Suddenly she stiffened. No matter if Max made her feel protected, he was still a man. Maybe she was making the smallest steps toward him? If only she could be whole again. The world going crazy with hate wasn't going to help matters.

"Veronica, you're very pale. We all heard about the riots and killings in Louisiana, all over the south actually. You witnessed it didn't you?" The caring reflected in his eyes touched her and her eyes filled with tears.

"I saw more than my share, I suppose. I just can't talk about it. Maybe someday. Parker is an admirable man, but he's going to bring down a war right here on the ranch. I can't help but be afraid for you, for Bridey, and for me. If I could I'd go somewhere that people got along. Some place where color didn't matter and men couldn't take the law into their own hands. I don't think such a place exists."

Bridey started wriggling in her arms, and Max took the baby. Every time he showed Bridey love, Veronica felt a surge of love for him. He could have easily just walked away from her when she got off the stagecoach, but he hadn't.

"Max, I just wanted you to know I feel horrible every time I pull away from you. I admire you greatly, and I feel blessed to have you as mine. I just can't tell you why, yet. I'm afraid if I said it all out loud I'd break and there would be no putting me back together." Swallowing hard she stared into his eyes.

"I know something happened to you. I can wait until you feel up to telling me." He leaned forward and kissed her forehead. "It's fine."

She gave him a small smile. She knew it wasn't fine but she just couldn't. He wouldn't want her anymore.

After supper, she left the dishes and hurried across the

way to be with Georgie when the meeting took place. She was too nervous to stay inside listening.

The terror she saw on Georgie's face echoed her own fear. They sat inside and talked about their children until shouting could be heard. The cradle was big enough to hold both babies and as soon as they got them settled they flew out to the porch. Both Parker and Max stared at them probably hoping they'd go back inside. Too bad, the two women sat down and watched.

Veronica clasped her hands together to keep them from shaking. She'd heard it all before. The men who thought they were over reacting and thought the rest to be fools. There were some who shot off their mouths with nothing useful to say, and there were the ones who felt it an obligation to stop the hooded men.

It didn't matter in one way or another; everyone got tangled in such things. Unless the fact that Parker was a Captain of the Confederate Army made some type of impression on the troublemakers.

"What do you think about all this, Georgie? You grew up on a plantation, didn't you?"

Georgie nodded. "I did. The problem is that people actually think it a fact that they are superior to the ex-slaves. They were brought up that way. They thought of them as property, not as people. The government telling them what to think isn't going over well. It's such a mess." A sad look fell over her features, and she sighed. "My parents were convinced they were right but in the end their way of thinking got them killed. I was always getting in trouble for helping out the slaves where I lived. My kindness was paid back and then some. I'd be dead or raped if not for them. We worked together to survive the last year. Then the taxes were due and rather than money, the tax collector wanted favors of an unspeakable nature. I divided up anything of worth before I left. I wish I could have helped more, but I could barely manage to get myself out of Tennessee. I'm glad Parker plans to hire some of the men, but I'm not naive." She shuddered and absently rubbed her arms as though chilled. "There will be trouble. Keep your doors locked and a gun near you from now on. I'm going to have Parker get me a gun belt to wear. You should do the same."

About half a dozen men got on horses and left. Veronica didn't know them but she felt bad all the same. People had very strong opinions about what should and shouldn't be done.

"Now we have to take sides against Southerners. When will it all stop?" Veronica asked

"Surely the Union Army will put a stop to it all," Georgie said.

"I don't know about in Texas, but in a lot of the other states, the army didn't think it was their worry. It's crazy really."

"I have a bad feeling about this."

Veronica nodded feeling suddenly chilled. "Me too."

CHAPTER FIVE

*V*eronica had just tucked Bridey in and was walking out of the bedroom when Max came into the house. He looked tired and worried but he grinned when he saw her.

"Would you like some coffee?" she asked.

He took off his hat and hung it on a peg near the door and then ran his fingers through his hair. "I would like some, thank you." He sat at the table, and she could feel the warmth of his gaze on her.

She'd never felt the way Max made her feel. Usually a man's gaze made her skin crawl but not Max's. He intrigued her, and he made her world feel safer. After setting the cups on the table, she sat across from him.

"I saw six men ride out. Did more leave? How do you know those six won't join the men with hoods?" She couldn't seem to stop asking questions. "Does Parker have a plan to have men keep guard at night? What about the cattle? He needs to guard those too."

"We could have used you in the Confederate Army. You think of everything." He chuckled for a moment and then grew serious. "The bad part about being far from the town is we couldn't nip this when it started. From what I've learned the men doing this are very tightlipped. Unless we catch them in the act we won't know who the perpetrators are." He paused, and his expression grew thoughtful. "Let's see, no, no one else left tonight. Yes, the six who left are very likely to join in on the violence. Parker is coming up with a long-range plan, but we do have a temporary plan to guard the ranch in place. The cattle have always been guarded. Anything else, my strategic wife?" He took a sip of coffee, and his eyes twinkled at her over the rim of the cup.

"Strategic? I was always told my ideas were stupid and to be quiet. You would have thought I would learn to keep my mouth shut, but I couldn't help myself. One time, my jaw got hit so hard I couldn't open it to eat." She widened her eyes as her heart dropped. "I didn't mean to tell you that; the part about my jaw that is. Oh, now I'm just rambling." She balled her hands on her lap, hidden by the table. He must think her an idiot.

"Veronica? You're not stupid, and your ideas are sound. I'd be pleased if you shared them with me. I'm sorry people were violent with you."

"It wasn't just with me. It seemed most of the men in that part of the county I lived in thought it their duty to educate women with their fists. I didn't suffer more than most."

"But you're afraid to have a man touch you." His voice was soft and his eyes were tender.

The truth was always the right path, but she just couldn't. "Aye, I am a bit skittish. High strung I guess." She wrapped both hands around her cup and stared at them.

"Did you and your husband get on fine? Did you have many arguments while you were married?" He gentled his voice even more. "Were you afraid with him?"

She took a deep breath and let it out very slowly. "I…

we…" She glanced out the window before she fastened her gaze on him. "I never lived with my husband. We'd been pledged to each other by our parents when we were young. Harvey was leaving to go to war, and the night before his mother got hysterical and demanded we get married. She wanted an heir in case…" Veronica stood and checked on the fire in the cook stove. She banked it like Max taught her. Finally, she turned back around. "All the younger men were leaving, my pa included. And there was a great amount of merriment going on, and when I was sent to find my husband, he was, well it was obvious it wasn't me he was interested in. I always knew Harvey was mine but he wasn't mine. He was loving another when he should have been making me his wife. I was too heartbroken to say a word. I left without being seen and spent the night in the woods. I couldn't go home and I couldn't go to his parents in case he never made it there. Which he didn't until it was time for him to leave. He went into his house, grabbed his belongings, and left."

"I'm so sorry."

"I asked discreetly if he'd looked for me that morning but he hadn't. I had to write to him. It was my duty but he never wrote back. I never really knew him. If I had I would have known about the girl he had. He'd promised to marry her. Harvey was killed a year into the war and the truth came out and I was blamed for not being woman enough to hold on to my man." Memories came surging back, and the humiliation came with it. "I would have thought the girl he'd been with would have been the one to carry the shame of it all but they hung it all on me. I was told that no one wanted me and I'd spend my days as a lonely widow that no one wanted to be seen with."

She took her cup to the sink and rinsed it out. "I'm so tired, Max. I'm going to bed. Bridey will be up for her feeding soon enough." He knew her first fall from grace, and he hadn't said much of anything. It didn't bode well for when she told him about Bridey.

MAX RAN his hand over his face. What a mess! He'd bet anything that more than just that Harvey and the girl he was having relations with had known what was going on. Small communities seemed to have a way of knowing everyone's business. Heck, her parents might have known. It sounded as if no one stuck up for Veronica. A married girl with a wedding night spent alone in the woods. There was nothing sadder. What happened to the girl who easily gave herself to Harvey? His jaw tightened. How humiliating it must have been for Veronica to have been blamed for Harvey stepping out on her.

Veronica was too young to carry such a burden. If only the war hadn't happened. Then again in her situation, things might not have gone too differently for his wife. *Wife.* He'd never given having one much thought.

A rifle shot crackled through the air, and he jumped up, grabbing his own gun. He rushed into the bedroom, and a lump formed in his throat at the utter fear on Veronica's face. "Get on the floor." He grabbed the rifle he kept near the bed and handed it to her. He then lifted the drawer with Bridey in it and put it next to Veronica. "Stay here. I'll be back, and no matter what stay away from the windows." Her face was stark white. He hesitated to leave her, but he didn't have a choice. He kissed her fast and hard and ran from the house.

It was pandemonium with dust flying and horses running everywhere. All the stalls and corrals were open, and he thought he saw a whip mark on a few of the horses racing by.

It took all his skill to dodge and weave to get to Parker's house.

William Cabot, the foreman, had the cowboys rounding up the horses. It was chaos.

"Captain, are you thinking this might be a distraction?" Max asked as Sandler and Willis joined them on the front porch. They had all served Under Captain Parker Eastman in the Confederate Army along with Walter Green who hustled up the steps.

Parker nodded. "It's exactly what I was thinking. Willis, tell Benny to guard Mrs. Maxwell. Green, go inside and guard Georgie, Sondra, and my son. We have enough men on the range."

Willis and Green went about their assignments with urgency.

"What are they distracting us from?" Max asked impatiently.

"The land! The land we set aside for the freed slaves!" Georgie yelled from the door.

"Get back where it's safe!" Parker yelled. Then he sighed. "She's right. Let's ride."

Their personal horses were well trained and stood near the barn apart from the muddle of horses. The soldiers ran to them, quickly saddled their mounts, and off they went. Max wasn't even sure where the land was located. They followed Parker. One of the men who'd left must have passed on the plans for the land to whomever was behind all the trouble.

Max wasn't positive, but he didn't think anyone was living on the land yet. As they got closer they saw flames but it wasn't the land that was on fire. His stomach clenched when the burning wooden cross came into view. They slowed and dismounted before they got close. With well-trained eyes they searched the area from where they stood.

Parker signaled for them to move forward. They moved

in sync slowly until they reached the circle of light given off by the fire. A dead man with a rope around his upper torso was lying on the dirt.

Max covered the ex-slave with his bedroll. They'd seen it all in the battles they fought in the War Between the States, but this was horrifying. The man had been dragged behind a horse probably all the way from town.

"Why bother to light the cross if they thought we couldn't get to our horses?" Sandler asked.

Parker shook his head. His eyes were full of disgust. "They know we have plenty of men on the range. They wanted their handiwork to be spotted. It might be for the best if we backed off. I can't help but feel this man's death is my fault. We stirred up trouble."

"No, this is not our fault." Max said empathically. "We wanted to put an end to the terror. This would have happened tonight anyway just in some other place. They hide behind their hoods and think no one can touch them. I have a feeling this will be going on for a while but maybe we can at least try to find out who is in charge."

"Everything is so backward," Willis said. "We supposedly fought to keep slaves most of us didn't have, and now that they are free, there is no one to protect them? What is going on in that Washington place? Isn't that what that government is supposed to do? I don't understand any of this." He kicked the dirt. "I never held with slavery. But it seems to me the President's right hand doesn't know what its own left hand is doing. Is it any wonder these men committing these crimes aren't afraid of being caught? What if we do find out who they are, will it even matter? The Union Army is turning a blind eye to it all. I'm all for what you want to try to do, Captain but it may cost us everything to do it." Willis took off his hat and wiped the sweat off his forehead with his sleeve.

Parker's lips formed a grim line. "You're both right. I can't abide this type of violence especially toward people who can't defend themselves. But at the same time we might lose everything we've worked so hard for. It would be easy to stand back."

"But we never go the easy way," Sandler said with a smile.

Parker smiled back. "We never have before. Let's go back and make sure everyone is accounted for. Then I'll send one of the men with a wagon to pick up the body. Like it or not, we're involved. We'll need to take the body to town tomorrow, and I'll let it be known we will not allow this to happen again on Eastman land. I think we might want to rethink where we build houses for the married freedmen. We'll need them closer to us, I think. Georgie thought perhaps they'd want their privacy, but you know what? Why don't we ask the men we hire what they'd like?" He swung himself into the saddle. "Let's ride!"

The condition of the dead body kept flashing through Max's head. That man suffered something awful. Some of the Southern men felt as though the freedmen were taking their jobs and land. The ex-slaves didn't have anywhere to go, and they weren't given much, if any, help to start new lives. Those men in Washington weren't using the brains God gave them. Now more would suffer before it was all said and done. *Please God, protect the freedmen.*

He didn't know what was right or wrong anymore. Protecting his family and the ranch were his priorities. Why couldn't the atrocities have stopped when the war was over? He felt gut kicked.

They returned to the ranch house, and Parker sent a few cowboys to go get the body. Max was glad when one of the cowboys offered to take care of his horse. He had a powerful need to see his wife.

He took the porch steps two at a time and turned the

knob, but the door was locked. He lifted his hand to knock but the door swung wide open. Veronica was in his arms so fast he smiled in amazement. He hugged her and then took a step back.

"Thanks, Benny. It helped knowing my family was in such good hands."

Benny, a seasoned cowboy simply nodded, grabbed his hat, and quickly left.

"He doesn't talk much," Veronica said. She started her gaze at his toes and made her way up to his face.

His lips twitched. "Well, what do you think?"

Her smile lit up the whole house. "You're in one piece." She walked to him again and surprised him when she wrapped her arms around his waist and sighed.

Without hesitation, he enfolded her into his embrace.

"When will it ever end?" she whispered. "When will we be able to lay our heads at night without worry? I was hoping that Texas would be that place."

"I'll keep you safe, both you and Bridey. Is she sleeping?"

"No, she's found her feet."

Max unwrapped his arms and turned toward the bedroom. He took Veronica's hand and together they walked in to see Bridey. She lay in her drawer cooing as she grabbed her feet, then let them go, only to grab them again. She smiled as though she was proud of her achievement. Then she spied Max and her eyes grew wide and she reached out a hand to him.

Leaning down to lift her, his heart expanded as never before. She gave him a smile and grabbed his ears and refused to let go.

Veronica looked like she was trying not to laugh, but she lost the battle and her light laughter was nice to hear, but he needed his ears back. Bridey had a strong grip.

"Help me before she wrenches them off."

"Here give her your finger to grab instead."

He did just that and eventually she switched from pulling his ears to tugging his fingers. And she smiled at him again. "I see how you are, young lady. You think your precious smile allows you to do whatever you want. I'll tell you a secret… you're right." He kissed her loudly on the cheek.

Veronica tried to take her from him, but Bridey refused to let go of him. He sighed. The baby was good for his heart.

"Will her father ever try to lay claim to her?"

Veronica paled and looked unsteady. She sat on the bed, appearing shocked.

"I didn't mean to pry. It's just that she's stealing my heart, and I guess I wanted to be sure she won't ever be taken from me."

Veronica stared down at her hands for a minute. "No, he's dead. It might be a sin, but I'm glad he is. I'm also glad Bridey looks nothing like him." Her voice was bitter.

"I'll be a good Pa to her," he vowed.

Veronica gave him a faint smile. "Good, because she seems to have lost her heart to you too. I do thank you more than you could possibly know. I was sure she'd have a life of being called all sorts of names. We certainly got lucky the day I saw your ad. I have to admit I saw the ad at a neighbor's house and stole the newspaper. I felt horrible about it, but I had a notion I should write to you. I've slept with a rifle in my bed for far too long. It was time to start over."

"It's a brave thing to pack up and leave for the unknown," he commented softly.

"It would have been cowardly to stay. Men started knocking at my door again since Bridey was a bit older. It would happen again, and I couldn't take the chance. I never did get much sleep."

He was about to ask her what would happen again, but Bridey began to fuss and then cry. She was a loud baby.

"Here, let me feed her then get her to sleep." Veronica laughed. "You've never been that close to her when she screams, have you? You should see the look on your face."

His cheeks warmed, but it did his heart good to hear laughter. Veronica had led a hard life, and he hoped to make a better one for her. "I'll give you some privacy. It'll be bedtime soon enough." He left pulling the door closed behind him.

It would happen again, and I couldn't take the chance. Had someone forced himself on her or had she willingly taken a lover? Loneliness was a powerful thing that could lead a body down the wrong path. As nervous as she sometimes grew when he got too close, he was leaning toward thinking she had been forced. He'd just have to wait for her to tell him. Was the father really dead?

A SMILE TUGGED at Veronica's lips as she smiled down at Bridey. She was a precious baby and Veronica was lucky to be her mother. Maybe she should have been smart and changed their names so no one would find them, not that anyone cared. It would be out of spite if she were found.

She was glad that Bridey looked nothing like her father. It made him easier to forget. Well, most of the time anyway, except at night in the dark. Nightmares plagued her but hopefully now that they were safe, they'd stop. They'd been less severe and she hadn't woken Max again.

After feeding Bridey, she put her new soft nightgown on. It even had a pink bow at the top. She'd never had anything so fine, but she'd need to talk to Max. He must have spent a fortune on her and he needn't have. She didn't expect fine things. A roof over her head and food was all they needed. Stroking the material again, she smiled. It was like a dream.

She got into bed and pulled the covers up. Max would demand his rights soon. She'd have to clench her teeth and endure it without trying to fight him off. Maybe he wouldn't notice anything was wrong. From what she'd heard, most women didn't like that part of marriage anyway. She didn't know all that much about it except it was painful. Maybe Max didn't like it either. That might be wishing too hard, though. Men must like it. Saloon girls were popular for a reason.

It had been a long day of worry, and her eyes were drifting downward when the door opened. She couldn't help but gaze at him. He had such big shoulders and a nice hard chest. He had the lean, strong body of a soldier. A lazy smile graced her face before she realized it. She corrected it with a frown.

"I liked your smile better. What's the frown for?" His right brow cocked.

"I shouldn't watch you get undressed. It's not ladylike."

He chuckled softly. "It's perfectly fine if the man is your husband. I know your first husband was a cad but I promise you, I'll look at no other woman the way I look at you. I was raised to honor my wife and to provide for my family. I don't think it'll be any hardship to honor my vows."

Tears misted in her eyes. "I don't think I've ever heard kinder words. That and the way you want to be Bridey's pa… I feel blessed. For so long, I thought perhaps God had forgotten me. My problems weren't as important as many others. Waiting and praying paid off." One tear rolled down her face followed by another.

Max climbed into bed and pulled her to him. With everything in her, she tried not to fight him. He laid her head on his shoulder and loosely held her. It took her a bit, but finally she relaxed against him.

"Did it ever go off?"

"What?" she asked.

"Did the rifle ever go off when you slept with it?" he teased.

"Yes, it shot a hole in my foot."

"You don't have a hole in your foot."

She laughed. "Didn't you sleep with yours out in the field?"

"Yes, and one of the greener soldiers did have his go off. Luckily it only put a hole in his canteen."

She put her arm around his middle. "I didn't think about it. I didn't…really a hole in his canteen?"

"It's a cautionary tale." She could picture Max smiling.

"One you made up."

He hugged her to him. "You're too smart for me. Go to sleep."

It actually felt pleasant to be in his arms. He was nice and warm, and best of all she felt no danger with him. She actually had a moment of serenity before she fell asleep.

She woke when Bridey cried to be nursed, and for a moment, she didn't know where she was. She stiffened feeling arms around her, and her heart raced. Her whole body shook before she got ahold of herself and eased out of Max's embrace. She was a hopeless coward.

She smiled at Bridey as she lifted her and received a sleepy smile in return. She changed her diaper then sat back on the bed and fed her. After a few minutes, her face warmed. He was watching, she could feel it. Sure enough, she turned her head and Max had his eyes wide open. The flair of desire was in his gaze, and she almost hadn't seen it.

She turned her attention to the baby. How was she supposed to feel? Part of her liked what she saw in his eyes, and part of her was deathly afraid. Bridey must have felt how nervous Veronica was; she didn't fall asleep but kept eating for a change.

After she finished feeding Bridey, she rocked for a bit until the baby fell back to sleep. She didn't want to go back into bed. Could she put her head back on his shoulder? The comfortable feeling she'd had with him earlier had disappeared. What was she supposed to do? She walked out of the bedroom and stood at the front window with her arms wrapped around herself. If she couldn't find a way to control her fear, she'd lose Max for sure.

All her doubts crept back in. She shouldn't have married him. She was only cheating him out of what a marriage was supposed to be. Her chin dropped to her chest, and she closed her eyes. She wasn't any good at pretending. Max was the type of man she could so easily love, but it would hurt too much knowing she failed as a wife. Even if they did have relations, she might not be able to have children. It was another lie she heavily shouldered. They kept piling on until there were days she'd thought she'd break from the weight of them.

She heard him and then felt the warmth of him behind her.

"Please don't touch me. I'm having one of my moments where I can't bear the thought of anyone touching me." She sniffled as tears fell.

"Come sit on the sofa, and we can talk. I haven't told you much about my childhood, and I know you want to hear about it."

She was grateful for the hint of humor in his voice. Turning away from the window, she followed him to the sofa and sat down next to him without touching him. Despite her best efforts to stop them, a few tears still fell.

"I grew up not too far from here. We had a very tiny farm. We raised mostly what we needed and hunted for our own food. My father trapped and made money from pelts. I caught a few horses and built a corral. I found that I was good at breaking them. I was able to help the family out. I had a sister, but she was taken by the Apache we believe. No one saw it but from the unshod hoof prints that's what everyone seemed to think. She was ten, and I never saw her again. But from what I hear, they make the children they take part of their tribe. I hope that was the case, and she didn't or doesn't still suffer.

It broke my parents' hearts, and somehow the blame was put on me. I wasn't even home that day. A few days later, I went and checked the traps, and when I got home, my horses were all dead. My father had a big grin on his face and a jug of moonshine in his hand. I went into the house, grabbed my things, and left without saying goodbye. That has always been my one regret, not hugging my mother goodbye." He sighed and looked thoughtful for a time.

"I joined the Confederate Army. Almost every young man was doing so. It was an exciting time. We were all so full of ourselves and thought we'd beat down those Yanks in a matter of weeks. I was barely seventeen, old enough to be on my own, but there were plenty of times I wished I could just pack up and go home. About a year in, I found that my parents had been killed by outlaws. That's what the sheriff's note said. I haven't even been back to see if they're buried there.

The one thing that kept me going, or rather the one person…was Parker. He showed me that a man could be a good and effective leader without resorting to violence. Violence had been my pa's way. I might have been that way if I hadn't been taught by Parker that there was another way. Quick with his fist, my pa was. He was that way toward my ma and sister too. I've spent my life trying not to be my father, and I'm proud of the fact that I've never felt the violence inside me he must have had."

If she could have, she would have reached out to him to

reassure him, but she still felt undone. "You have succeeded, Max. You are so gentle with me and with Bridey. You're a good man."

"But not every man has been gentle with you, have they?"

"No, they haven't. My mother and father died, and it was just my sister and me. She married and I lived with them, sharecropping. It was not a happy marriage, sharecropping only made us poorer and of course I was the embarrassment of the county. My sister Hester became with child and turned her husband Amis away from their bed." She stood back up and didn't know where to go or what to do. The back of her throat ached, and she couldn't tell him. She couldn't even bring herself to look at him.

Staring at her feet she whispered, "I can't tell you the rest."

Max stood and tried to put his arms around her but she pulled away.

"I thought I could tell you. I'm so sorry. It's not that I don't trust you." Her shoulders shook as she sobbed.

Max came close to her but didn't touch her. "Honey, I understand. You don't have to tell me. But if you do, I'm here to listen. I would like for us to go back to bed. I can sleep as far away or as close as you like. I don't mind holding you when you cry. I have a feeling not too many people had enough consideration for your feelings."

His eyes were filled with concern. Nodding, she walked into the bedroom and waited for him to join her in the bed. Her body felt frozen in place for a while, but eventually she moved a couple inches at a time and then laid her head on his shoulder. She sighed as he put his arms around her. The anguish inside her would never go away. Max deserved a better wife.

CHAPTER SIX

*V*eronica tried to smile as Georgie took delight in the purchases Max had made.

"He's a good husband. I know he had good taste. He had to go and get dresses and the like for me and everything was much more than perfect." She picked up the doll and hugged it. "This is the sweetest doll." Then she gave a gentle sigh. "Everything will work out for the two of you. I really believe that."

"I hope so," Veronica said without enthusiasm.

"Is something wrong?" Georgie asked. She frowned and tilted her head.

"No. Yes. I don't know what to do. I'm afraid to let him be a husband to me. I don't want to be touched that way. But I don't mind if he watches me nurse Bridey. I think I'm a whore, except I've been treated in a way I can't stand to lay with a man." Veronica tried to swallow back her torment. "I know it makes no sense."

"You were married before."

"We never—he left to fight in the war right after the wedding. I was married, then widowed yet untouched."

"Was the birthing of Bridey so bad you don't want to have another baby?" Georgie asked softly.

She didn't want to talk about births. "I was attacked and badly hurt. I don't want anyone to know. I tried to tell Max, but I just couldn't. He must already think badly of me arriving with a baby. I know the town is talking about me. I've brought him nothing but shame."

Georgie took her hand a squeezed it gently. "Max isn't like that."

"I just wish I had somewhere else to go. I can't do this. I can't be married." She heard a noise and realized that Max had just walked in. How much had he heard? His jaw tightened and his eyes narrowed.

Georgie hugged her. "I need to get back to Douglas. Everything will be fine." She touched Max on the shoulder as she left.

"I'll find you a place, a safe place and we can have the marriage annulled. I didn't realize just how unhappy you were with me." His voice was bleak. He stared at her for a moment and then left.

Her heart plummeted. What had she done? Everywhere she went, everything she did was a disaster. She couldn't blame others anymore. It had to be her. She wasn't pretty enough, wasn't smart enough. Harvey proved that. She wasn't loveable or desirable. She certainly wasn't respected, the knocks on her doors by men proved *that*. Everyone had such a low opinion of her, they thought she seduced her sister's husband despite being beaten so badly she couldn't walk for days. What was it about her? She obviously brought it all on herself, but how? It'd be best if she lived her days alone, but how would she do that? She could take in wash, she supposed. Men would start knocking on her door again. She shivered as the misery of it all encased her.

She didn't have it in her to try to start over in another

town. What was the use? Bridey began to fuss, but she'd been fed not long ago. Veronica picked her up and held her, she sang to her, she rocked her, and she walked back and forth with her in her arms, but nothing worked.

She spotted Max at the corral and marched outside. Without a word, she put Bridey in his arms. He looked startled, but Bridey stopped crying.

Yes, it was her. Perhaps she had a bit of the devil in her that others could see. Her father had certainly told her that enough times. With tear-filled eyes, she left Bridey with Max and ran back to the house. Once there she lie across the bed and sobbed. Her heart felt as though it had been ripped out, but it was her fault. It was *all* her fault. There simply was no other to blame.

She must have fallen asleep. Dusk had turned everything gray when she opened her eyes. It was the silence that worried her. She got off the bed and walked into the sitting room. No one was there. She was alone, just as she should be. Bridey would be better off with Max, and Georgie could nurse her.

Impulsively, Veronica packed a bag for herself with a few of the clothes Max had bought her and some food. She peeked out the window and didn't see a soul, so she put on her cape and went out the front door and then hurried to the back of the house. She'd find a place for herself somewhere. She entered the woods and aimlessly walked.

Bushes tore at her. She stumbled over some rough terrain and fell against a rock. Her palms began to sting as she caught herself against the trunk of a tree to keep from falling to her knees.

MAX THANKED Georgie for the meal and then lifted Bridey from the cradle she had been sharing with Douglas. "I need to go check on Veronica. She's had enough time to herself, I think."

"She's a good woman, Max," Georgie said kindly.

"I know. I just wish she'd confide in me. I also know whatever happened wasn't her fault. She has a good heart. We'll get it all figured out."

"They sure didn't tell us how difficult it was to be a husband. Not one married soldier said a word about it," Parker said. He laid a hand on Max's shoulder. "You'll be fine."

Max smiled. He felt a bit more hopeful for his marriage. "Thanks for the support."

"Now, if you need any tips on how to—"

"Parker Eastman! That's private between a man and a woman." Georgie tried to glare at him but ended up smiling instead.

Max carried Bridey across the yard. He chuckled, thinking about Georgie. He'd do what he could to make Veronica just as happy. The house was dark. Maybe Georgie had already gone to bed. She'd need to feed her daughter soon.

But he knew as soon as he walked into the house something was amiss. His heart beat faster as he went from room to room looking for his wife. He thought it a longshot, but she could be using the privy. He started to go back outside, but he backtracked and looked in the bedroom instead. He scanned the room and sighed. Some of her clothes were gone. There was an imprint across the mattress as though she had lain there before she left.

He sat on the bed feeling lost. Surely she wouldn't have left Bridey? He got up and headed outside to the privy just to be sure before he took Bridey back to Georgie. What in tarnation was Veronica thinking? There was so much danger lurking about, and she'd up and walk into it by leaving.

Georgie quickly took Bridey after he walked into their house. "Where is Veronica?"

Max rubbed his hand over his face. "Some of her clothes are gone. I guess she left us."

"Oh, Max."

"Let's saddle up. Georgie you'll take care of Bridey?" Parker asked as he buckled his gun belt.

"Of course. Don't either of you worry. I'm sure as Veronica realizes how dark it gets out there she'll be back."

"I hope so," Max said, but he wasn't convinced.

Max saddled the horses while Parker told the men to look for her around the ranch and to keep an eye on Georgie and the children.

Max's chest constricted. She'd left him, she had actually left him. He took a deep breath and let it out slowly. What did she think would become of Bridey? She couldn't have been thinking clearly if at all.

Parker was waiting in the yard when Max led the horses out of the barn.

"There aren't signs that she left on horseback. She didn't walk down the dirt road. The only foot prints of hers I can find are from your house to mine and back and one set around to the back of your house. But it's all woods back there."

Max frowned. "It looks as though we're going through the woods." If she'd cared for him, she wouldn't have left. His heart hardened with each step he took.

———

HER HAIR WAS CAUGHT up in a tree branch and it hurt like the dickens trying to get it untangled. Finally she grabbed a knife out of her bag and cut the hair away from the tree. She could run and run, but she couldn't run away from herself. She needed to head back. Everyone there already thought badly of her. She would learn to live with that.

Too bad she was lost. A wolf cried nearby, sending a shiver down her spine. She kept walking until her feet hurt. She wasn't familiar with the area, so she was clueless as to where she was. She broke through the trees onto a tilled field and gasped. Across the field men on horses carrying torches formed a semi-circle in front of a cabin. They were yelling vile things, trying to get the occupants to come out.

It was the hooded men! Instinctively, she ducked back in the woods to hide, but she turned back around and watched. The men broke down the door and dragged a family of ex-slaves out. She was so focused on what was happening, she never heard the horse until she was dragged up and lay across the front of the saddle face down.

It was near impossible to breathe let alone scream. The man wore white cloth over his clothes. She saw his dark trousers and horse dung-covered boots. Fear kept her still. She needed to wait for the right moment to try to run. He rode back to the cabin and threw her on the ground in the circle of men and next to the screaming family.

There were two men and two women along with three small children. This was going to be bad, and she'd end up dead, she was certain of it. Trying to get up would be useless so she stayed on the ground.

"I told you we had a spy. It's her. She's the one who has been following us night after night," the man who captured her announced.

"I'm not so sure. She has a baby. She'd be nursing half the time," a deeper voice said. Laughter followed.

"Where's the kid now?" demanded the first man as he

dismounted and grabbed her up to a standing position. He ripped her bodice. "She needs to be taught a lesson."

Bile filled her stomach. She knew what came next. Would it only be the one man or would the others want to have a turn? She trembled as tears trailed down her face.

"No one does a thing unless I say so," a third man said. He looked to be tall from her perspective.

He must be the leader she mused. His horse was a thoroughbred, and his boots had a very nice shine to them. They would probably never be seen with dung clinging to them. Swallowing hard, she started to silently pray. This was no poor ignorant bunch of men.

"Then she belongs to me!" the man who had captured her said.

"Let's get to what we came here for," the leader ordered. "Men, put the nooses around their necks."

"Not the women, right?" another man asked in a hesitant voice.

"We can let the women live. They won't be making more babies with dead negroes."

The screams got louder, and the wailing and begging started as soon as the rope nooses were around the men's necks and their hands were tied behind their backs.

Veronica turned her head and threw up. She felt faint but wiped her mouth with the back of her hand. "You can't do this. It's murder! If you leave now, we won't say a word to the law."

Her kidnapper backhanded her across the face, drawing blood. And when she opened her mouth again he slapped her to the ground. Once on the ground he kicked her repeatedly. "Keep your mouth shut."

The women and children huddled together, as the ropes were thrown over a large tree limb.

Veronica closed her eyes as her skirts were being shoved

up. Once again she was in an impossible situation of her own making.

The crack of gunfire split the air, and she rolled away from the wicked man getting ready to undo his trousers. She frantically tried to get her skirts back down, but her hands wouldn't cooperate. The hooded men scattered, and the men with the guns raced toward them. There were only two of them, and she finally managed to roll so she was on her stomach. Her skirts weren't up as much in the back. She just wanted to die.

Her heart was grateful that no one had been killed. She got up on her knees, holding her bodice to her and then struggled to her feet and tried to just walk away. The sound of hooves behind her terrorized her and she dropped and then curled into a ball. She was too young to die. She wanted to live.

"Veronica, it's me. It's Max." Suddenly, he was crouched next to her.

She slowly opened her eyes and lifted her head. "Max? Oh, Max. You should ride on while you can. Trouble follows me wherever I go. I'm no good. I never have been, and I shouldn't have come to Texas."

"Sweetheart, let's get you home. We can talk about it later. Right now I want to hold you in front of me on my horse and know that you are in one piece."

"I'm sorry. You and Parker shouldn't have bothered looking for me, but I'm glad you did. You saved that family."

He helped her up, and the anger in his eyes when he saw her ripped dress caused her to step back in fear.

"I didn't ask for it. I didn't tease the man. I just walked out of the woods. This dress was very respectable before that man…"

"Of course it's not your fault. Come I'll put you up on the horse."

She sat on the horse and watched Max go and talk to Parker. Max came back, mounted up behind her, and they rode toward the ranch. He put his arms around her and pulled her back against him. He didn't say a word, and she was grateful.

He guided the horse right up to their house, jumped down and carried her inside, and then gently put her down on the sofa. "I'll be right back. I need to send more men to that house."

His gentleness confused her. Anger, yelling, hitting...she knew what to expect when a man did those things, but kindness made her anxious. Maybe he was being nice before he told her where he was going to ship her off to. Again, that would be a problem of her own making. She was a bad seed just like her brother-in-law Amis had often called her.

Her shoulders sagged while she still held the two halves of her bodice together in one hand. She'd left Bridey. How could she have done such a thing? She didn't even understand her actions. She was tetched in the head for sure.

MAX STOPPED to let Georgie know what was going on and she insisted on keeping Bridey overnight. Max gave her a sad smile and thanked her. He stood at the bottom of the porch steps to his house. He didn't know what to say or what to do. His heart ached almost beyond bearing. She had run away from him. Would she have ever come home on her own?

He stared up at the half-moon wishing he could put their cares off until tomorrow, but he couldn't. It wouldn't be good for either of them. He needed to know why, if she'd tell him. He wanted her and Bridey to be happy with him. *Lord, what am I doing wrong?* He had never felt so low or so doubtful in his life.

He sought deep to find his courage to talk to her and walked up the steps and into the house. She sat with her head hanging as if in shame.

"I'll make us some tea." He busied himself putting water on to boil. Then he walked to the sofa and dropped to one knee. "Do you have any injuries I need to tend?" He stroked her hair back from her face. He wanted to love her, but she'd break his heart even more than she had already.

When she didn't answer, he helped her into the bedroom and very gently removed her clothes. She had a few nasty bruises. There were several on her arms and one big one on her shoulder and several more on her back. He covered her with a nightgown and carried her back to the sofa. If he put her in bed she'd fall asleep before they talked.

The water was boiling, and he made them tea. He put both cups on the table in front of the sofa. He wanted to sit next to her but chose to sit in a chair across from her instead.

"Why did you leave?"

"I've not been able to be a good wife to you," she said so softly he had to strain to hear the words. "And it hurts my heart so. Then today, after you said you would move me out, get our marriage annulled…no matter what I did, Bridey would not be comforted until I put her in your arms." A tear welled in her eye and slid down her cheek. "I thought you'd both be better off without me. The truth of it was so strong I just had to leave. It ripped my heart out, but I knew it was what I had to do. I can see by the expression on your face you don't understand."

Max moved to the sofa and took her hand. "I just wish you thought you could have come and talked to me about it. We all have doubts about ourselves. I've found it best to talk it out. You've told me a bit of your story, but I think if you told me all of it, I'd have a better understanding."

As much as she didn't want him to know, it was time to

tell him the whole sordid story. "Are you sure? You'll feel differently about me and not in a way that would be good."

"I care about you, and you're my wife."

Her hand seemed so small in his, and he did make her feel safe. "Get comfortable. It's a long story, and I should have told you from the first."

He gave her hand a quick squeeze before he put his arm around her and pulled her close enough for her to rest her head on his shoulder. She played with one of his buttons on his shirt before she began.

"I told you about my sister turning Amis away from her bed. He'd been walking in on me dressing whenever he could get away with it. I know Hester saw him, but she never said a word. In fact she implied it was my fault. I took to dressing under the covers while still in bed."

She swallowed over a lump of emotion then pressed on. "There was more work to do than ever. Sharecropping doesn't mean the workers get an equal share. If we made enough to keep ourselves fed and warm through the cold season, we were the lucky ones. Amis loved his moonshine, and we'd just been told our share was to be even less that year. He was enraged, and I was his target. I'd heard him slap Hester around and he'd been quick to backhand me when I made a mistake or said something out of turn. I would have left but there wasn't a door open to me. That night he had his way with me. I wanted to die. He hurt me so much. Then he laughed about me being a virgin. He also beat me so bad that night, and I could hardly walk but he made me work the next day. I had a black eye and there were bruises all over, but not one person said a word."

She needed to catch her breath. She half expected Max to jump up and leave but he stroked his hand up and down her arm.

"He continued to have his way with me and I was stupid, I

kept fighting him. I should have just lain there and let him but not me. Hester still never said a word and that hurt me more than all the cuts and bruises. I mean even though she was afraid of Amis she could have told me how sorry she felt for my plight. She acted as though I was the one who was wrong. I was in constant fear and Amis thought it was funny. I became pregnant.

I was raised to believe that every child was a blessing. I didn't tell him. I wasn't sure what he'd do, but I knew it wouldn't be good. Hester knew, she had to have known with all my morning sickness, but she didn't mention it. She glared at me when I brought her meals to her in bed. She decided she needed to stay in bed leaving me to do even more work. I did it, though. If I was working I wasn't being beaten.

One day I went to the church for help, but even the minister thought I was the problem." Tear began to fall. "How do you tell a woman who had a broken nose that it was her own fault? Months went by and it was obvious I was with child and Amis still didn't say anything until Hester complained about it saying he had shamed her. She was near her date. Amis still didn't say a word about my child to me. Then one night he threw me on the ground and beat me until I lost my baby. Hester had her daughter the same night."

Veronica couldn't sit anymore. It was all too much. She stood and began to pace. "No one was there to help Hester. Amis didn't go for help, and I couldn't get up off the floor. Finally, I gathered what strength I had, crawled into Hester's room and tied off the cord and cut it. Hester was dead, and the baby was crying.

I took the girl and held her to me, and she was looking to feed. Yes, I was that far along. I held her to my breast and she fed. I mourned for my son and fed my niece at the same time. I was still bleeding so I grabbed some of the diapers Hester had made and packed them inside of me. I washed Bridey and dressed her. I wasn't sure what Amis would do when he got back.

He finally came home. He had to get the doctor since Hester was dead, and the doctor was kind enough to take care of me. Amis kept yelling he wasn't going to pay the doctor for tending me, but the doctor didn't care. In fact, he told me to get myself gone as soon as I could and to take the baby.

I healed slowly because I had to work the fields and tend to Bridey, and the house and meals were mine to take care of too. I gave the first letter to the doctor, and when I got your letter with the ticket I had hope for the first time in forever, but I knew I'd lied to you. You have to agree I'm not good enough for you, Max. Now the whole town of Spring Water is talking about us, and how shameful I am to bring a child who wasn't born in wedlock. There is something about me that makes people think I'm not worthy of love or respect." Stopping in front of him, she dared to look at him, expecting to see disgust on his face but the tears in his eyes were her undoing. She sobbed and when he pulled her down onto his lap she sobbed some more. It was as though she'd never stop but she couldn't help herself.

"How much you have suffered with your sorrow, shame, and abuse. Go ahead and cry it all out. I'm so sorry you lost your son. The shame isn't yours to bear my sweet girl. You are a good wife and mother. I can wait until you're ready. What about Amis, though? Won't he be wanting his daughter?"

"I didn't lie when I said the father is dead. He lost enough blood there was no way he survived. Amis owed men money and they broke down the door. One of the men shot Amis. They pointed the gun at me, but I was holding Bridey and I thanked them for killing him. They were so surprised, they left. I packed that day and I left too."

"Bridey is lucky to have you...as am I."

"I thought for sure you'd turn me out. You are the good one, Max."

"No more running away. You were attacked tonight, and even though he didn't... You were still beaten. Let me get you tucked in."

She searched his eyes for any sign of revulsion, but she only saw tenderness and sadness.

Max carried her to the bedroom, pulled back the covers, and set her on the bed. He covered her with the quilt. "I'm going to go get Bridey. You'll be all right for a minute? There are men guarding both houses."

She nodded and watched him leave. Her body hurt something awful and she was spent emotionally, but she no longer feared her secrets. She no longer feared he'd turn her out. But she didn't believe it wasn't her fault. Too many people had told her it was.

CHAPTER SEVEN

$\mathcal{M}$ ax swung the ax over his head and hit the wood with a hard thwack. It split and went flying in two directions. He wanted to stay close to home for a few days. Veronica needed to heal both inside and out. This morning she was calmer than he'd ever seen her, and he didn't think she could enjoy Bridey more than she already had, but there was a serene smile on her face when she interacted with the baby. Veronica even smiled when he held Bridey. She had numerous bruises, and he told her to take it easy, which of course she ignored. Finally, he threatened to tie her to the bed. She was sitting on the sofa sewing when he came outside.

He felt bad that he was shirking his duties on the ranch, but Parker laughed and told him he worked too hard as it was. Parker was going into town or rather past the town to where the freedmen lived to talk to them to see about hiring some on. He also wanted to know how they felt about living on his land.

Max felt as though he should go and have Parker's back, but Sandler and Willis went with him. Green was guarding the house as was Max. He had his gun belt on and his rifle close at hand. There would be revenge for their interference last night, he hadn't a doubt about it.

The family refused to leave, so Parker sent rifles out to them. Max didn't think it would be enough. They'd have their house burned with them in it and their crops trampled before it was done. That's what soldiers on both sides had done to many farms and plantations. But he could only hope they'd be successful in protecting themselves.

There had to be a way for them to all live in peace. President Johnson wasn't any help at all. He'd never wanted to end slavery in the first place. Then there were generations of people who were brought up to believe that being white meant being better, smarter, and more deserving. It was going to take a lot to make a change. People were often stuck in their ways.

Max chopped more wood. He didn't have any answers. Parker was going to bring a whole lot of trouble on them, but in his opinion, Parker was doing the right thing. They'd need more guns and more ammo. They should probably build more line shacks for guards to hole up in come bad weather.

Perhaps they wouldn't want to come and work on a ranch owned by an ex-confederate soldier. Veronica was watching him out the window again. He grinned to himself. He could feel the heat of her gaze. Telling him the whole tragic story, and then the long cry that followed seemed to have cleansed her in some way. Whatever it was it seemed helpful. Veronica had slept peacefully last night in a way he'd never seen her do before.

Finally, he turned to the window and his lips twitched as she backed away. So she didn't want to be caught watching him. It was time to go back inside. He'd exerted enough inner anger on the wood. How could people have allowed what happened to her? How could they have blamed her for that darn Harvey's cheating? It didn't make any type of sense but people did think it was a woman's fault if a man strayed.

He walked into the house. "Glad to see you resting," he teased.

"I didn't do any work."

"No, you just watched me chop wood."

Her face became fiery red. "You're very strong. I've chopped more than my share of wood, but mine never went flying so far after it split."

He smiled widely. "Complimenting me? I like it."

"Take off your shirt." She walked toward him.

This time, it was his face that heated with embarrassment. "What?"

"I want to measure you for a new shirt. The one you're wearing pulls too tight when you swing the ax. That's why I was studying you for so long." She carried string to measure him.

He laughed. "And I thought you were amazed at my muscles." He unbuttoned his shirt and glanced away as he took it off. He didn't want her to think he had anything other than a shirt on his mind, but it was hard.

Her gasp brought his gaze to hers. Her eyes were wide and filled with fascination. She took a step forward with the string but then she took a step back and her expression became one of confusion.

"Maybe I could just use one of your shirts to measure and make it a bit bigger." Her words came out slowly.

He put his shirt back on and buttoned it. "It doesn't have to be done today, honey. Like I said last night, I'll wait. One step at a time. Right now, just seeing you smile at me is such a gift. Come, I want to press a wet cloth against your eyes."

She dipped her head. "I must look a fright."

"You'll always be the prettiest gal in the world to me."

"You hit your head, didn't you?"

She sounded so serious he frowned. "Now, why would you think that?"

"You think of me as pretty. I'm many things, but pretty isn't one of them." She quickly put her string back into her sewing basket. Bridey started to fuss and then cry until Veronica lifted her out of the drawer.

"I was working on something in the barn. I'll go grab it and finish it up in here." He didn't wait for a reply. He hurried to the barn and got everything he needed to finish the cradle. He'd wanted to surprise Veronica with it finished, but he suspected she'd be just as happy to watch him finish it. He hustled back and realized he felt happy to spend time with his wife and daughter. He didn't care that Amis and Hester were Bridey's parents because they weren't really. Not in any way that counted. Veronica was the only mother the little one had known and he was proud to know he was the only father she'd known or would ever know. She was his daughter.

"Oh, Max, you didn't need to go to the trouble." Veronica's eyes teared when she saw the cradle.

"No crying, now."

"They are joyful tears. Oh my, I don't think I've ever had tears of joy before." She bit her lip and then smiled, lighting up his whole heart.

"It's no trouble, she's my daughter after all. And I plan to make you cry joyful tears whenever I can." He set all he carried on the kitchen table, leaned down, and gave her a light kiss on her lips, and then gave Bridey one on her cheek. It hadn't occurred how close he'd be to her uncovered chest. He quickly stood and concentrated on relaxing his suddenly tightened jaw then went to work on the cradle.

He'd meant what he said about waiting, but it was going to be a bit harder than he imagined.

IT GLEAMED and it felt so smooth to the touch. Her mouth opened in awe as she inspected every inch of it. "It's the loveliest thing I've ever seen."

"I hope our daughter has many a good sleep in it," Max replied, his voice filled with pride.

She swallowed hard, afraid to hope. "You said our daughter. Do you mean that Max?"

"Of course I do, and I feel it even stronger now that I know the whole story. She's ours and I don't care what anyone says. Talk will die down soon enough. We'll raise her and give her brothers and sisters."

"God willing. The doctor wasn't sure if what Amis did to kill my baby caused any damage, but he didn't see anything obvious. I'd like to have your child someday. But in order to have a child we'd need to…" She wasn't sure where to look. She didn't want to see the expression on his face. She wanted to try, but she wasn't sure she'd ever be able to bring herself to allow a man to touch her, even Max.

He snaked his arm around her waist and pulled her into a hug. "Let's not think about it or mention it for a while. I don't want it between us. I feel so close to you, let's not ruin it with regrets and unfulfilled wishes." He kissed her forehead. "Now let's put a wet cloth on that eye. I bet you hurt all over."

"No one ever cared how hurt I was before." Tears welled, stinging her already painful eye, and she blinked them back. "I was always expected to go on about my work. Everyone would take a good look at my battered face, and then they'd pretend not to notice anything. I guess no one wanted to go against Amis. The poorer farmers…we all mostly ended up as sharecroppers and mostly kept to ourselves. The sheriff knew what was going on, but by his way of thinking, it was a family squabble. I was property, owned by my father and then by Amis. Harvey would have owned me if he hadn't gotten himself killed." She couldn't help the sigh that escaped her.

"I don't own you, honey. We are partners in our life as husband and wife and as parents." He wet a cloth and led her to the sofa then sat her down and took a seat next to her. Fresh pain seared her eye when the cloth hurt went on, and she hissed.

"I know it hurts. Try to set your head back against the sofa for a bit. I wanted to discuss something with you. Are you happy here, or would you like to head west and get a piece of land all our own?"

"If owning your own land is something you want, I'll go with you of course, but I'm just as happy here." She squirmed, trying to look up at him, but the angle was too awkward. "I can't see you. Are you happy with my answer, or are you scowling?"

He chuckled. "I'm happy here, but if you wanted to start new where no one knows about Bridey, then I'd go and carve out a new life for us."

"You have to stop being so nice to me today. I'm not used to it, and I'll end up crying joyful tears all day." A few tears leaked out under the wet cloth. "Georgie and Sondra are the first real friends I've ever had, and I'd like to stay."

"Then stay we will. Rest for a bit, and I'll get us something to eat. After that I'm fixing you a nice warm bath to soak some of the soreness out of you." He moved away from her, and she felt the loss of his body touching hers.

She puzzled over it while she measured the cradle, grabbed the material she needed, and then quickly sat back down. She measured and cut the muslin for cradle ticking. "I don't know what else you need to do to finish the crib. It's so beautiful."

"I want to rub it with beeswax to make it shinier. You'll see when I'm done that it was worth it. Haven't you ever…?"

"No, except for the one the Eastman's have. We always used drawers or sometimes baskets. Theirs isn't as glossy."

"That cradle has been used by the Eastman family for generations. Usually between children you sand it down and wax it again to make it look new," Max answered as he made griddlecakes.

Nodding, she threaded her needle and started on the ticking. There was a large bin of chaffed straw in the barn to stuff the ticking with, but she probably wouldn't be allowed to leave the house to get it. It was just as well, she'd probably never make it that far. She was hurt worse than she had admitted, but she didn't want Max to worry. He'd already been too good to her.

"Here you are, my sweet. I'm betting you like syrup on your griddle cakes."

He put a plate on the sofa table and then poured syrup over them.

"Don't put too much on, syrup is a luxury," she said. He was using it recklessly.

"We always have more than enough syrup. We barter our beef for goods not just money. I'll show you where those items are kept."

She popped a piece of the syrup-covered griddlecake into her mouth and sighed. "This is heaven. What else do they have?"

"There's coffee, tea, canned fruit, and mostly things that couldn't be had during the war. The shipments have been coming in, since people now need beef. The traders know what value we expect for the cattle, and they bring it. Sometimes it's a lot of syrup. It's better than sending the cattle up north and getting paid what they decide is the right price. We do send some that way too just so we can keep our little system in place. I think next we're going to ask for material and school books. Georgie is determined that a school be built in these parts soon."

"See what can be accomplished when people work together?" she whispered, awestruck. "It's amazing."

"Yes, it is. Finish up while I make sure we have enough water heating. I'm going to have Georgie come and help you."

She raised her brows. "Why?"

"I thought you'd feel more comfortable plus I'd be out for blood looking at your bruises again and I can't leave the ranch at the moment." He gave her a wry grin.

He tried to sound lighthearted about it but she knew he meant it. "That's a good idea. Could you ask her if I could use a sliver of her pretty smelling soap?"

He kissed the top of her head. "I certainly can. I'll clean up later." He checked the hot water reserve and put more water on to heat. He took his hat from the peg. "I'll get her."

She swallowed hard. How did she end up with such a loving man? Well, to be honest, she reminded herself that he never mentioned love, but he was certainly caring. There was so much love in her heart for him and it terrified her. He said what people thought didn't matter but she knew better and it kept her from being wholly happy. She finished the ticking except for one end. She'd sew that closed after Max filled it.

Georgie had a huge smile on her face when she came through the door. She hurried to the sofa and gave Veronica a kiss on the cheek. "I'm so glad you're safe. I was beyond worried when you were missing and hysterical when I learned you'd been hurt. Next time just ask me and I'll plan your escape."

Max cleared his voice loudly. "I don't think she'll have a use for your services, Georgie."

Georgie gave him an impish smile. "Of course not. I just couldn't take worrying like that again is all."

"I'm sorry I worried you. Thanks for coming."

"Not a problem. Max, get the water poured please. I just put Douglas down for a nap but you never know with that baby. There is no set pattern I can figure out with him. Growing up, I seem to remember babies were put on a schedule but not my stubborn boy. I'm hoping when it happens the next one will be as darling and sweet as yours."

Max poured the steaming water into the tub and set a towel on a chair he'd moved beside to the tub. Then he set a pail of water he'd just pumped next to the tub. "Yes, I agree our daughter is a sweet pea. I'll be on the porch if you need me." He started to leave but paused and looked over his shoulder. "Honey, do you need me to lift you into the tub?"

"I can do it." She blushed, and he grinned.

When he finally left, Veronica slowly walked to the tub. "Georgie, I'm going to need more help then I told Max. I can hardly move, but I buck up when he's around."

Georgie's mouth formed an O. "Let's get you undressed." Georgie gasped when she saw all the bruises. Tears filled her eyes. "Are you sure you can get in?"

Veronica clenched her jaw and slowly and painfully got into the bathtub. She eased herself down and nothing had ever felt so wonderful. "Oh, this makes me feel better already. It was foolish of me to run off, Georgie, and I promise I won't leave again like that. I was—it was—I thought he'd have me and then kill me. They had white hoods and white material over their clothes. If I had come from this area, I might have been able to figure out who they were. The one in charge had an expensive horse and boots. The man who caught me wore old boots covered in dung and his saddle had seen better days."

"I'm so sorry you had to go through what you did. He didn't kick you in the ribs did he?"

Veronica winced as she touched her ribs. "Yes, I supposed he must have. He kicked me and it seemed as though he was never going to stop. Why?"

Georgie handed her a cake of scented soap. Veronica put it to her nose and inhaled. "Lavender?"

"Yes and it's yours to keep."

"I couldn't possibly—"

"Veronica, there is little pleasure for women here in Texas, allow me to give you one."

Georgie's smile was a smile of a friend, and Veronica's heart squeezed. "Thank you."

"The reason I asked about your ribs is with the kind of bruising you have, they are either cracked or broken. But let's you get clean and then let you soak a bit before you get out and I look you over."

The lather of the soap was blissful. "I had a sister, but she never once was kind to me. Here you are having only known me a short while, and you've been more of a sister than she ever was."

"Don't get me to weeping. I think many of us feel the exact same way. Most of us lost our families in the war, and now the friends we make, they become family. Now hush so I can wash your hair."

A strange sense of relief went through Veronica. She wasn't alone anymore. Of course she had God and he'd been her only family for a long time but it was nice to have actual people as family too.

"All rinsed. Let's get you out of there and dried off. I'm going to have to ask Max to lift you. You shouldn't be moving until those ribs are wrapped. I know you didn't want him to see exactly how hurt you are. Didn't he check you last night?"

"Yes, but I only showed him my shoulder and part of my back."

Georgie gave her hand a quick squeeze. "It'll be fine."

Veronica watched as Georgie went outside. She could hear their raised voices, but they quieted before they both came inside. She tensed, waiting for Max to scold her, but he gently lifted her and carried her to their bed.

"Do you want me to move the wee one?"

"She might wake if you move her. I'll try not to scream."

Max nodded as Georgie bustled in with a roll of bandages. "I'm not exactly sure…" Georgie whispered.

"I can do it." Max touched each rib and his frowns were as bad as the pain. "Oh, Veronica, why didn't you tell me? Putting the bandages on will hurt bad, but in the long run it'll hurt less than earlier today. Max started wrapping her ribs, and he wrapped them good and tight.

It felt as though all the blood drained from her face. It was hard to breathe, and the pain was bad. She'd suffered more before, though, so she would get through this. Gritting her teeth, she kept her cries in. She thought the worst was over and she planned to lie back on the bed, but Georgie stepped forward and began to rub ointment on her shoulder and back. A sheet had been laid over her bottom half, and the thought of them looking anywhere else for bruises was too much to bear.

Georgie must have sensed something. She bent and kissed Veronica on the cheek. "I need to get back, but I'll check in with you tomorrow. Feel better."

Before Veronica had a chance to say thank you, Georgie was already gone. When she turned her gaze to Max she could see he planned to take the sheet off of her, and he was sorry for it. Tears filled her eyes and she bit her bottom lip. He helped her lay back before he uncovered her.

He said something under his breath, and she would bet it was a curse.

"The man kicked me a lot."

"Why didn't you say so last night?" There was no patience left in his voice.

"I should have, and I really don't know why I didn't, except I didn't want you to grab your gun and go after those men. I was ashamed that I'd been attacked."

"Did he?"

"No, he only kicked me down there and it hurts."

He shook his head and grumbled. "The insides of your thighs are full of bruises."

Grimacing, she forced herself to meet his gaze. "You didn't expect me to allow him to open my legs without a fight did you?"

"Maybe he wouldn't have hurt you so much."

She widened her eyes. "Do you know how many men kick their wives out of their homes if they are soiled that way? No, I will not allow another man to do that to me ever again. I'd rather be dead then have someone take me by force. I'm a survivor, but that doesn't mean I can go through it again. It was bad enough I had to suffer the terror of it all."

With his lips clamped shut, he gently put ointment on her legs. Then he grabbed a clean shirt. "Here, this will be easier to get on you instead of a nightgown. You are an amazing woman, and I'm so sorry this happened to you. Now, get some rest."

Would he kiss her before he left the room? He was busy gathering up the ointment and bandages, and she didn't think he would but he stopped, bent over and gave her a long leisurely kiss. Then he sent her a loving smile.

As long as she lived, she'd never figure men out. He had the kindest, most forgiving heart she'd ever known. He hadn't once said it was her own fault or that she was asking for it. He was more concerned about her than what others might say. No man had ever treated her like a prized treasure the way he did. Most of all, he didn't want her to leave, and that made her heart sing. She'd stay and build a life with her wonderful husband.

CHAPTER EIGHT

he next day, Walter Green and Sondra stayed with Veronica while Max went to see Parker and Georgie. What had Parker learned in town? Had he learned anything that would give them a clue as to who was behind all the violence? Max also needed to remember to thank Georgie for all the care she had given Veronica.

Parker opened the door as soon as Max's boots hit the porch. "Glad you're here. We have a lot to talk about. I want Georgie in on the conversation since what we decide might change our lives and it might not be for the better.

Max tipped his hat to Georgie before he took it off.

"Max, come sit down. I just made coffee for us." She made a sweeping gesture with her arm toward the chairs in front of the fireplace.

He sat and thanked her when she handed him a cup of steaming coffee. Parker did the same. They waited until she had at last taken her seat.

Parker's mouth formed a straight grim line. "Is Veronica all right?" he asked.

"As well as can be expected. She'll heal physically, but it's not the first time it's happened to her and she's been through hell." He sighed, his heart still heavy. "But she finally told me her whole story, so I think we're on the right path."

Parker nodded. "Good. There wasn't a word about what took place. I have a feeling some of our good people of the town are responsible. I felt as though I was being watched. I rode out and went around to the other side of town where some shacks are set up, a kind of shantytown. They named the place Liberty. I don't know how long they'll be able to stay there. It wouldn't surprise me if someone sets fire to the whole place." He placed his cup on the table and stretched his arms in front of him.

"I talked to many living there, and it's split down the middle. Some just outright don't trust me because I'm white. Others are willing to grab hold of the dream of a house to live in and real work to do. Right now, I have ten confirmed new hires who have families. They'd like them to be near enough to the house to have protection but far enough so they can have their own community."

"They don't want to have anything to do with us?" Georgie asked. She frowned and her shoulders sagged. "I want to know the families that live here."

"I knew that, and I asked a man named Darrius, who is their leader, about it. He said as soon as they realize that my wife and the other ladies don't treat them as servants they'll be friendly. I understand they are suspicious and think I want free labor. I don't blame them in many ways. I'm going to order the lumber for their houses if you both agree this whole thing might work out. I have to warn you what Max and I saw the other night was evil and violent. Those men could easily start a war with us."

Georgie momentarily paled as she sat quietly for a moment. "This is our land and we can do with it what we want. I do think it's a good idea to train everyone—women included—how to defend ourselves. We're going to need a whole lot of rifles. I don't want any harm to come to them. What happens after the ten come and realize we're good people?"

Parker rubbed the back of his neck with one hand. "I think Max might agree that we need as near as even numbers of black cowboys and white cowboys. I don't want fighting within our ranch. Some of the men have different talents, one is a blacksmith and another's a carpenter. Some of the women can help to make a huge garden to feed us all. We'd all have to help in all the efforts. I want them to have input along with our people to see what we can come up with. I have a feeling we won't be welcome in town. What we can't make for ourselves, we'll get in Fort Worth."

Max started to talk but stopped and allowed Georgie to go first.

"Certainly you don't think that the store owners in town will give us trouble. You made it possible for many of them to keep their businesses open."

Parker leaned forward. "It's not the owners, it's what the hooded men might do to the owners. If I end up ordering the lumber I'll privately speak to the ones I can trust. If we can figure out a safe delivery system then we will."

Max sipped the last of his coffee. He put a hand on each knee. "We need to round up the cattle and bring them closer for a while. If we're less spread out, the easier it'll be for us to protect one another. If we put the new houses in that pretty valley, we'll surround them with cattle so it won't be easy to get to them without someone setting up an alarm. It'll take a bit of planning, but it's doable. And like any other ranch, if someone causes trouble they're escorted off the property. I think it worth it to try to help some of the ex-slaves. We've made soldiers out of some pretty questionable material, we can show them how to cowboy."

"Questionable material?" Georgie's lip twitched.

Parker chuckled. "We had this scrawny kid who ended up in my company. I don't think he'd ever seen a horse or a gun before. In fact, he was convinced he was afraid of horses. I was ready to send him to another unit when Max took pity on the kid and made him a first class soldier."

"What happened to the young man?"

Max laughed. "I do believe you know Walter Green."

Her jaw dropped. "But he's quick and strong, and I know he could protect me."

Max stood up. "He's come a long way. Though I may have to step in and teach him how to ask a woman to marry him. He's been courting Sondra for a long while now."

Laughing, Parker shook Max's hand. "I already offered. He wants to do it his way."

"Let me know if you need me. Georgie, thank you for all you did with Veronica yesterday. It was a big help. I'd best get back to my two girls."

He walked across the yard to his house with a smile. *My Girls.* They certainly are my girls and one of these days, Veronica would realize it too.

Walter's face was bright red, and he looked a mite uncomfortable while Sondra was holding Bridey. Veronica's lips twitched. Good thing he arrived in time to interrupt their torture of Walter.

"What mischief have you two ladies caused?" Max asked with merriment in his voice.

Veronica gave him a wide-eyed innocent look. "I have no idea what you're talking about."

She wasn't as pale as she'd been, and that made his heart smile. "I'll take my daughter." He gently took Bridey from Walter. She scrunched up her face, and he was ready for her to wail but she examined him, gazing into his eyes, and smiled.

"You have her practically purring," Walter teased.

"Looked as though she was plenty content in your arms, Walter," Sondra said as she gave Walter a pointed look.

Walter stood. "Sorry to have to run off, but I have plenty to keep me busy. Miss Sondra would you like me to escort you back?" he asked in a very formal voice.

Sondra stood and gave Veronica a kiss on the cheek. "Miss Sondra is it?" She walked by Walter holding her skirt so it didn't touch him at all as she purposely glanced away from him. She was out the door in no time as Walter scrambled to catch up with her.

"It looks as though you had a fine time," Max commented. "I'm surprised he hasn't asked for her hand yet."

"All in good time, I suppose. Do you need anything?"

She crossed her arms and narrowed her eyes. "All in good time. Is that because he wasn't part of the bet?"

"Did they like the cradle I made?" He needed her to think of anything but the bet.

She tapped her foot. "I do remember Sandler and Willis mentioning some bet on our wedding day, but I was too nervous about you accepting Bridey to think much of it. Now I find out you never planned to marry. You never wanted a wife, but you did want a house and you did want to beat out Sandler and Willis. You married me because of a bet?" She looked both mad and anxious.

He sighed and sat down. "You already know. I needed a bride, so I put an ad in the papers. It's as simple as that. I hoped for the best, and I ended up with the best. End of story." He smiled down at Bridey and stroked her soft cheek with his finger. She reached out and grabbed his finger and tried to bite it.

"That's right Bridey, bite that man for his scheming ways. Now I know why you took us both on. You didn't think you had time to find another wife. I knew it was too good to be true. I'm far from anyone's idea of a proper woman and bringing you a baby born on the wrong side of the blanket too. I'm sorry you got stuck with us." She stood and took Bridey in her arms. Veronica stared at the front door, and he knew she was thinking about leaving.

He let out a breath he'd been holding after she went into the bedroom, slamming the door behind her. Next he heard Bridey cry briefly. As hurt as she was she wasn't going anywhere for a while.

He put coffee on to boil while he tried to figure out what to do. She'd been abused all her life and told she wasn't good for anything. Deep down, or actually not too deep, she still believed it. Weren't they making progress? He could have sworn they were. She had acted as though she trusted him.

He poured himself a cup of coffee. She had no idea she was worthy of love. Stunned by the direction of his thoughts, he put his cup down with a thud. Love? Did he love her? He cared about her and her happiness. Aw, heck, he hadn't planned to fall in love, but he'd gone and done it.

He sat at the table and took a sip of his coffee. Now what? He ran his fingers through his hair. If he told her he loved her now, she wouldn't believe him. He made some willow bark tea that Georgie had given him to help with Veronica's pain. Not once did Veronica bring up how much pain she must be in. She probably got hit for it in the past.

He'd better figure out what he planned to say to her. But where to begin?

VERONICA WATCHED Bridey sleep in her cradle. It had been hard to breast feed her with the tight bandages. She'd been hurt like that before, though. Had she had cracked ribs before? It was more likely than not. The pain of her body was nowhere close to the pain in her heart.

She didn't know a thing about good men or kind men. She thought Max really liked her. She had felt a closeness with him. He made her feel safe and a little bit loved. Too bad it had all been an illusion. He did love Bridey, of that she was positive.

She shook her head as tears fell. A bet, she was just some stupid, insulting bet. She'd heard about it before, but it hadn't sunk in until Sondra went on and on about it. Max kept saying how lucky he was. Yes, he got a new house and a daughter. If only he hadn't given her hope for good marriage. She was used to being a thing people used without thought.

It was though her dreams had come true, and then someone woke her up calling her a fool. Oh, she'd get over it. She always did and then she'd just cook and clean and be a wife and mother. Bridey loved her, and she'd just hold on to that.

The door opened, and she stiffened. He'd be mad at her. She kept her gaze fixed on her hands, afraid to see how Max really felt about her.

"I brought you some willow bark tea. It's for the pain." He sat on the bed and handed it to her.

"Thank you."

"I know you're upset, and yes I wanted the house, so I advertised for a bride. But I'm glad I ended up with a woman I can be friends with and a daughter as sweet as Bridey."

She lifted her eyes and studied his face and he looked sincere. "I've never been friends with a man. I didn't know men would even consider a woman for a friend."

"I'd like to think we're friends. We get along and I enjoy having you here. You're a kind woman and I like you. I like knowing you're here when I come home. Both you and Bridey."

"It is a very nice house. I'm just sorry you got stuck with a woman who is full of shame. You must know I'm not good enough for you. No matter where we go, people will be whispering about me. I know you said you didn't care but how can you not?" She sipped her tea.

AT LEAST THAT'S how Sondra had made her feel, that she wasn't good enough, that Max deserved better. Oh, maybe she hadn't meant to be mean, but the woman sure had judged and found Veronica lacking.

"You've done nothing to be ashamed of, and I don't care what others say. I care about us getting along. If you answered someone else's ad who knows who you would have ended up with. I could have gotten unlucky and ended up with a shrew. We both took a gamble, and I think we both won."

She wanted to grab onto his nice words but she was frightened. "You don't have to be nice to me. I have nowhere else to go. I won't be leaving."

His eyes opened wide. "Oh, honey, that's good because I don't want you to leave."

"I know, because of Bridey."

His brow furrowed. "What does that mean?"

"You are quite taken with her. I see the joy on your face when you hold her."

"She does have me wrapped around her finger, but I'm taken with you too."

The conversation was going nowhere. She wanted to believe him, but something held her back. Was it just her own fear? She sighed. Why couldn't she trust?

"I wouldn't have changed the fact that I can nurse Bridey because of what happened to me, but as for the rest I wish I had come to you clean and pure. All I know is that doing my wifely duty will hurt and I'll end up with my soul squashed." Her voice shook, and she drew a ragged breath in an attempt to steady herself. "You need a woman who would welcome you with open arms. I'm afraid that woman will never be me."

Sadness settled over his features. "Veronica, part of me wants to yell at you and tell you just how wrong you are and another part of me wants to hold you and kiss you until the fear goes away. One thing for sure, I refuse to allow you to be afraid of me. I'll sleep in the other room from now on."

"See?" Her stomach dropped. "Now I've chased you away. You are my husband, and I want you here with me. I will try my best to be accommodating."

He stood and this time his eyes flashed with anger. "Accommodating? I need to get some fresh air before I say something I'll regret. Do you need anything before I go?"

Watching him was too much for her, and she turned her head away. "I'm fine. Please don't sleep in the other room." She hated how desperate she sounded. Her sense of dignity had been shredded a long time ago.

"I didn't mean to say that," he admitted. "I wouldn't want to be anywhere else but beside you. Now before you tell me I'm wrong, I'll get that air."

When she turned her head back, he was gone. This was all her fault. She had let herself get hurt over a stupid bet. She should have kept her mouth shut and her feelings close. When would she ever learn? She needed to practice self-preservation or she'd end up either homeless or dead.

MAX WALKED to the corral and put one foot up on the first wooden slat of the fence. Taking off his hat he slapped it against his thigh. He'd just jammed it back on his head when Sandler came and stood next to him.

"Sandler, if I was a swearing man I would string all the words together and have at it."

"I take it you're mad." Sandler smiled.

Max took a deep breath and let it out slowly. "No matter what I say, it comes out wrong. Not wrong exactly, but my words are taken the wrong way. If anyone ever mentions the bet again, I'm going to have to slug him."

Sandler snorted. "Problems with the missus? Maybe losing was a good thing for me."

"You know, we went through a lot fighting those Yankees. We saw things that still give me nightmares, but we came out of it reasonably fine. Veronica wasn't even close to any fighting, but she's more scarred on the inside then most soldiers." Emotions welled in his chest. "Her family life was bad. I'd say they were all pure evil. Hitting and beating women was a daily thing, and the women had nowhere else to go. How did things ever get to be so bad? When did people become so evil?" Max looked up to the sky. *Lord help me.*

"I think there has always been evil, Max. But the good outnumbers the bad. Veronica unfortunately encountered too much evil. Was her family church going people?"

Max shrugged and glanced at his friend. "I don't see how they could have been, but I think everyone has known a person who is only Christian in church but not out of it. I'll ask her. It might heal her heart to go to church. Not this week though. She has broken ribs."

Sandler frowned. "From the other night? I didn't know she'd gotten hurt so badly."

"Neither did I until morning. She grew up having to work the fields no matter how much they beat her. She's afraid of men." He shook his head as a wave of sadness swamped him. "I just don't know what to do anymore."

"Max, what do you do when a horse has been beaten and is skittish?" asked Sandler, one eyebrow raised in query.

Max shrugged, not understanding what the other man was getting at.

"You have to have patience and make sure the horse knows you'll never hurt it. Go slow with her. You'll have a lifetime together, and the time you take now to allay her fears will be worth it." He made it sound so simple.

"You're right. I've been doing just that. Thought we were making progress. But Sondra and Green mentioned the bet and it set her off. She thinks she's undeserving of love."

Sandler nodded. "Then she ended up with the right man. You might not know this but you have a tender spot in you." He chuckled. "Not that you're not one tough soldier."

Max smiled. He turned and was surprised to see Georgie headed their way carrying flowers.

"She's upset, isn't she?"

Max nodded. "How did you know?"

"Sondra told me, and then I saw you out here hitting yourself with your hat. She cares for you. You have to remember that. I thought if you brought her some flowers it'd be nice. She's like a horse that's been beaten."

Sandler laughed. "I already gave him that speech."

"See? It's good advice." Georgie handed him the bouquet of flowers. "Go. I don't want her lifting the baby again."

Max took the flowers and kissed Georgie on the cheek. "Thank you both."

He looked up at the sky and whispered, "Thank you." He'd gotten his help. With a much lighter heart he went back home.

CHAPTER NINE

*V*eronica couldn't help but smile. She sat on the sofa with her feet up, and her flowers were on a table right next to her. She'd never had flowers from a man before. She touched the petals of the roses and smelled them. Once in a while, she'd rearrange them. Her fear of losing Max was gone.

He'd slept in their bed last night, and very slowly he had taken her hand. His palm was as calloused as hers, but his hand was much bigger with a sprinkling of hair on the back. He'd rubbed his thumb over her knuckles ever so gently, soothing her. She had drifted to sleep and awakened calmer than she had felt in a very long time.

"You don't need to babysit me all day," she said, coming back to the present and the man sitting across from her. "I'm fine."

Max smiled. "I'm babysitting my daughter. You're not allowed to lift her."

His smile warmed her.

"Did your family ever go to church?" he asked.

"We sat in the second pew until my parents died. I never did understand how they could smile and say all those 'amens' and then slap us across the face an hour later. My ma said it was the way they were raised. I don't know if I believe that. I have never had the urge to hit Bridey."

"Bridey is perfect, that's why." His face grew serious. "I'm glad you're able to start over with me. We don't believe in hitting women around here. You'll get more comfortable with me by observing what I don't do. I'm letting you know, I plan to court you until feel undying love for me or like me."

She chuckled. "I think liking you will be easy enough. Thank you again for the flowers. They are so beautiful. I never knew flowers could make me so happy."

He grinned at her. "I'd like to think it was the giver of the flowers that made you happy."

Her face heated and Bridey cried just in time.

Max went into the bedroom and came back with a freshly changed Bridey. Boy, Max had the magic touch. Bridey just cooed and smiled at him.

"Is it just Bridey and me who succumb to your charms, or is it all women?"

Max cocked his left brow. "So you think I'm charming. I'm off to a good start." His smile went all the way to her toes. He settled Bridey in her arms and went to put supper on to cook.

The cook stove still fascinated her. They could make it so the heat was low enough to cook both the meat and vegetables without charring one or the other. It was absolutely amazing. She couldn't wait to experiment with it. She switched Bridey to the other side.

"Max, I'm sorry about being so upset with you. It was just a stupid bet, and you didn't even know me. You must think me the type of women who jumps to conclusions and finds trouble where there isn't any." She spoke loudly.

There was no answer, and her shoulders sagged. She was out of her element. She didn't even know how to apologize the right way.

She held Bridey up against her shoulder and patted her back until she burped.

"Wow, she could measure up to the men in the bunkhouse with that loud burp," Max teased as he joined them.

Veronica couldn't help but laugh. "This little one is going to take on the world when she's grown."

He sat on the table next to the roses and gazed into Veronica's eyes. "You were right about one thing; it was a stupid bet, and I didn't know you. But you aren't the type that looks for trouble. In fact, you avoid conflict from what I've seen. My hope is someday you'll speak your mind without thinking you'll be punished for it." He grasped her hand and kissed it. Then he took Bridey. "She must hurt your ribs."

"It's worth it for her to feed. I never knew what love was until Bridey. She has brought me more smiles in her short life than I'd ever had my entire life. Now I have you, and you make me smile too." Her face heated at her confession.

Max bent and kissed her lips. It was the sweetest, most tender kiss she'd ever known.

"Well, Miss Bridey, what shall we do today? Your mama needs to rest. Horses? Why yes I can show you the horses. I happen to know a lot about them."

Bridey cooed.

"What was that? No you can't ride until you're a mite bigger. Maybe next month."

Veronica opened her mouth to protest and Max laughed.

"I'm only kidding. It'll be at least two more months. I'll get her blanket in case she needs it. We won't be long but honey, please try to rest."

"I will if you can bring my sewing basket to me."

"It's a deal."

Max got the sewing basket for her and the blanket for Bridey and off they went. She was still smiling after they left and that hadn't happened in her life. Max was a good man. She was glad she'd cut out the pattern pieces earlier. She'd get the dress done in no time. Then she planned more gowns for Bridey and a new shirt for Max. She'd ask Georgie about the yard goods for the shirt. All she had was dress lengths with flowers on them.

She pulled out the buttons and lace. She'd look like a fine lady, and could only hope she wouldn't feel like a fraud wearing it.

MAX SPENT a long while with Bridey in the barn, wanting to give Veronica plenty of time to rest. He snuck back into the house, and when he saw her sleeping on the sofa, her sewing basket with a neatly folded project resting on the floor next to her, he backed up and carried Bridey over to Parker's house.

Georgie welcomed them and took Bridey from him. "Parker was on his way to talk to you. Don't worry about Bridey. You two go talk."

Max furrowed his brow. What was going on?

"Max, I was on my way to see you," Parker said as he walked down the stairs. "Let's go out on the porch. I don't want you to scare the kids when you start yelling."

Max's stomach dropped. Whatever it was it sounded bad. He glanced at Georgie, who looked concerned, and then followed Parker outside.

They didn't bother to sit. Parker looked at Max for a minute. "I was in town today. Have you ever heard of a man named Amis Reacher? He didn't know your name but he knows your wife. Says she stole his kid. He said his son, so I don't know what this guy is doing. He has it in for Veronica and he intends to drag her home by her hair."

Max stiffened. "You saw him?"

Parker shook his head. "I heard it from Jamie Butcher, our neighbor to the east. This Amis fellow was spouting off at the Sink Hole last night. Jamie was playing poker, and he said the more Amis drank the worse his threats were. But no one said a word. They told him they'd never heard of her or the boy."

"How do you mistake Bridey for a boy?" Max took off his hat and slapped it against his thigh a few times. "That son of a…" He rubbed the back of his neck.

Then he sighed. Nothing for it but to tell Parker her story.

"Veronica doesn't want people to know, but you need to be apprised of the situation. Amis was married to Veronica's sister, Hester. Hester was with child and turned Amis away from their bed. Amis had his way with—well he forced— Veronica. She ended up carrying his baby too. He still beat Veronica despite her condition. Veronica's son was born dead after Amis beat her and Hester gave birth about the same time. Amis was busy drinking or something. Hester died, but her baby did not. Bridey lived." Max took a deep breath and let it out. "It was the doctor's idea to switch the babies."

Parker blew out a long breath. "Poor Veronica. No wonder she hates to be touched. We need to make sure this Amis doesn't know they're here. I'm not sure if that's going to be possible with the number of men in a rage because I hired freedmen."

Max stared at Parker. "You knew she didn't like to be touched?"

"She flinched at the wedding when I offered my congratulations, and she gritted her teeth as others offered theirs. Unless you've been taught to observe everything, it wouldn't be obvious. I doubt any others noticed." He shook his head. "She's certainly had a bad time of it."

"We need a plan," Max said.

"The corral is close enough to your place for you to keep an eye on her. From what Georgie said, Veronica should stay in bed for a few days."

"I shouldn't have left her alone to come here." Max turned to go back to get Bridey.

"Wait. Green is watching your house. There's no one better for the job."

Max relaxed his shoulders. "Green is a first rate soldier. Maybe I should take Veronica and Bridey away for a while." He stared at his house. Was Veronica resting still?

"Sandler and Willis will become regulars at the Sink Hole starting tonight. Amis sounds like a big mouth who tells everyone his business. Veronica knows how to use a rifle I imagine."

"Her parents were sharecroppers. They probably made her go and hunt for dinner. She's had a hard life and she doesn't think she's good enough for me."

Parker smiled. "You grinned at her, didn't you?"

"Why?"

"Women can't resist your boyish smile."

Max shook his head. "Did you just say boyish smile?"

"Those aren't my words. The belles from town have been known to have said it a time or two. I was glad no one brought one of those snobs back here to marry."

Max put his hat back on. "I can't keep this from Veronica. She needs to know the danger she's in."

"That would be for the best. Meanwhile, when you're working with the horses, Green will watch the house. Or if you want you can stay home for a few days."

"Thanks, Parker, but I have a feeling Veronica will insist I go. I can't leave her for too long, though. She's not supposed to lift Bridey."

"Have her close the shutters in the kitchen when she needs you. You're sure to see it."

"Good idea." He huffed out a breath. "I'm a bit calmer now. I should get back. Thanks for standing with me on this."

"We've always had each other's back, and we've been good at it." Parker clapped his hand on Max's shoulder. "Let's go get your daughter."

THE DOOR OPENED and Veronica put her sewing down and smiled at Max and Bridey. "I was beginning to wonder where you were. And why is Walter Green staring at our house?"

Max handed Bridey to her. As glad as she was to have them home, she noted concern on Max's face and frowned.

Max removed his hat and put it on a peg near the door. He then sat in a chair opposite her. A chill went up Veronica's spine.

"I have some news, disturbing news. Your brother-in-law is in these parts, and he's been asking about you all around town, especially at the Sink Hole."

She immediately felt lightheaded. "Amis is a-a-alive?" She must have heard him wrong. "Amis is here in Spring Water?"

Max stood and took Bridey from her. "You look as though you're about to be sick."

"I do feel a bit on the sickly side, but I'm fine. How is it he's still alive?"

Max shrugged, and she realized he would have no answers.

"Did he ask about Bridey?" She held her breath waiting for a yes or no.

"Not Bridey exactly. He's looking for you and his son."

Veronica closed her eyes for a moment. "A son? Did someone tell him I left with his son?"

"I wish I knew, honey. He seems intent on taking you both home with him."

"That's why Walter's been watching the house, isn't it?"

Max nodded.

"I should go to another town. Perhaps I can leave Bridey with Georgie? I don't know when I'll be able to come back and collect her." It felt as though someone was ripping her heart right out of her chest. Then the fear of Amis shot through her.

"You're shaking. I won't let him anywhere near you or our daughter. He obviously doesn't know what's going on. Why he thinks you have his son is a bit bewildering."

"He wasn't there for the birth of Bridey and the death of my son. He thought it funny we were both pregnant, and he often said he'd have two sons. I was afraid if I had a girl he'd throw her out into the forest. He never wanted to look at the baby and then he was shot. How he even tracked me this far is a mystery." She couldn't get the shaking to stop.

"Sandler and Willis will go to the Sink Hole tonight and see what's going on. Maybe they can convince him you've moved on."

"He probably spent all his money drinking and well, you know. I wouldn't be surprised if he didn't have enough money to go home." Dread gripped her gut. "Oh, no! He expects me to take my sister's place." She got up quickly despite the pain and ran outside. She stopped at the side of the house and vomited again and again. Then she leaned against the side of the house trying to find her courage. It seemed to have fled as soon as Amis' name was spoken. He would beat her to death this time. And what would he do to sweet Bridey?

She slumped against the house until she was sitting on the ground. She had to hide Bridey. There was no way that man would ever touch that baby. Amis was a crafty one, and despite Max's assurances, he'd figure out a way to get to both her and her daughter.

A shadow blocked the warmth of the sun. She glanced up and there stood Max.

"Let's get you inside, honey. Do you feel any better?" He reached out both hands, and she placed hers in them. He easily pulled her up and she was soon in his arms, leaning against his hard chest.

"Max, I'm frightened."

"I know." He tightened his arms a bit, but not so hard he hurt her ribs. "I'm here. We'll make sure no harm comes to you or the little one."

"Is Bridey in her cradle?"

Max stroked her back up and down. "Walter has her. Bridey likes him."

"She does?"

Max chuckled. "Bridey would have made her displeasure known."

Veronica pulled away. "You're right about that." She took Max's proffered arm, and they walked to the front of the house. Walter looked as though he was telling Bridey a story, and the baby watched his face as though she understood him.

"Thank you for watching Bridey," Veronica said. Max took the girl from Walter and carried her inside.

"I wonder what he was saying that kept her attention?"

Max grinned. "What he always talks about: Sondra. Whether or not he should wait to ask her to marry him. He has a big list why he should and an even bigger list why he shouldn't."

She gave him a tight smile.

"I hate to ask, but we'll need description of Amis so we

can spot him if he comes close to the ranch." They stepped inside the house, and Max led her to the sofa. "Here, sit down for a bit. I bet that bending you just did hurt your ribs."

She gingerly sat down. "A bit, I guess. He's a head taller than me and muscular; he's not fat or skinny. His hair is long to his shoulders—or it was—and he almost never washes it. It's light brown. He has blue eyes. He also has a small scar right above his lip where I managed to hit him once. If he's at the Sink Hole then he'll think he knows it all. It gets worse when he drinks. Keep the girls away from him, because he'll hurt them."

"That's a great description. I'll pass it along to the men in a bit. What about his crops? I would have thought he'd had too much to do to leave Louisiana."

Sighing, she nodded. "You'd think so. He probably doesn't know enough to grow anything. After Hester married him, we did most of the work. His pa was a sharecropper too, so you'd think that Amis would know at least something about it. The plot is probably full of weeds. He didn't care as long as he could afford moonshine and drink with a few other worthless men."

"He's bound to run out of money soon enough. When that happens he'll probably make his move." Max held Bridey against his shoulder.

"I think she's sleeping. You might as well put her in her cradle," Veronica suggested.

Amis…alive. How had he found her? It made no sense at all. He was as dumb as a rock. Had she let it slip out at any time? No, she was certain she'd kept her mouth shut. Very certain since her life depended on it. Somehow he had found out and that worried her. There had to be money involved somehow. Amis didn't even like children. But he had enjoyed abusing her. Her ribs began to hurt more than ever, and she realized her body had grown tense. Amis was too close, way too close, and she didn't have complete faith that Max and the other men could protect her.

CHAPTER TEN

*M*ax made breakfast, did all the morning chores, and finally put Bridey down for an early nap. It hurt to see the fear in Veronica's eyes. She'd hardly slept all night, and that had kept him up too. Walter was watching the house, and Max nodded to him as he made his way to the barn.

He'd told Veronica about the shutters and to close them if trouble came. He saw a small measure of relief in her eyes. Sandler and Willis were watching a horse walk.

"I think its knee is swollen." Sandler stopped the horse and squatted down to rub his hands up and down the horses' knee. "Yep, this one will need stall rest for a few days." He stood and turned. "Hey, Max."

Willis turned, and he had bags under his eyes. "We stayed at the Sink Hole most of the night."

"You didn't have to drink," Sandler scolded.

Willis shrugged. "I'd hardly call that drinking. It was more like sipping and listening.

"The man is plain loco," Sandler began. "He raged about someone named Hester for a bit then shed a few tears because she was dead and it was her sister's fault. Veronica had a duty to take Hester's place and bring his son back. He went on and on about her stealing his son before he ever saw him. Someone might just tell him in order to get him to be quiet."

Willis nodded. "He was a royal pain. I wanted to hit him over the head in the hope that he'd pass out. We only had one night's fill of him. I can't imagine what the regulars felt like. We need to get him out of there. Preferably out of the state."

"Veronica isn't a very popular name." Sandler mused, rubbing his chin. "He's bound to find out. Parker told everyone to keep Amis off the ranch by any means possible. He's going to get himself shot."

"Perhaps we should just kidnap him while he's passed out and leave him in another state," Willis suggested.

"The thing is, Bridey *is* his daughter. He was so sure he was having a son. But Bridey is Veronica's sister's baby. He has rights and that's what worries me," Max said angrily.

Both Willis and Sandler looked confused.

"But don't you have to have a baby to feed the baby like..." Crimson seeped into Willis' cheeks. "You know what I mean."

"It's not my story to tell but Amis beat Veronica so badly she lost her own baby. Hester died in childbirth, and the doctor there told Veronica to take the baby girl and get out of town. It's a tragic story all around, but please don't tell anyone about it." Max took a deep breath. "Veronica didn't sleep a wink last night. I guess we all went without sleep.

Sandler shrugged. "It wouldn't be the first time."

"He's right about that," Willis agreed. "Max, go on home. We have things covered here. I heard about Veronica's ribs, and she's basically defenseless.

Max frowned and looked around the barn. "If you're sure

you two yahoos can handle things." He finished his sentence with a smile.

"Yahoos? Now I know you're delirious from no sleep," Willis teased.

"We'll keep an eye out. You go on." Sandler gestured toward the barn door.

"You two aren't going to town again tonight, are you?"

Willis laughed. "No, not tonight. I think Sandler here might actually shoot the guy."

Max chuckled as he left but he grew grim when he saw Walter. "Thanks, Green."

"No problem. Best get in there. Veronica keeps pacing and looking out the window."

Max looked up to the heavens and shook his head. "I guess that's her idea of resting. We better get rid of this guy and quick."

He saw the curtains flutter as he walked up the porch and wasn't surprised when the door opened.

Her hair was a mess trying to escape the braid Georgie had put it in for her last night. The circles under her eyes were darker than he'd ever seen. He closed the door behind him and opened his arms and felt a surge of heat as she walked into them.

"I think we have different ideas of resting," he teased.

"I'm worried. More for Bridey than for myself. He must have done something back home, something bad. Otherwise I really don't think he'd be here. There are plenty of younger girls there he could get hitched to."

Pulling her closer would only make her ribs hurt, so he kissed her forehead. "That's a good idea. There might be a wanted poster on him. I'll let Parker know. He can send someone to the sheriff's tomorrow."

"Thank you." She rubbed her hands up and down both his

arms. "You make me feel safer. I never knew there were men like you in the world."

"Like me?" He cocked his brow.

"Fishing for complements?" She smiled and the fear was gone from her eyes.

"Always. No one as pretty as you ever said nice things about me."

"Not even your ma?"

He grinned. "Other than my ma. Let's be getting you back to sitting and resting. Bridey is taking a long nap."

"I fed her while you were gone."

"Veronica Maxwell, I told you to signal if you needed help."

She laughed. "Are you scolding me? She was hungry and I fed her. I did sit on the bed while feeding her though."

Leaning down he kissed her soft lips. Too bad her ribs were still hurting, he'd like to pull her close and kiss her senseless. But he put his hand to the small of her back and led her to the sofa. "Rest."

"Fine, but only for another day or two."

"Only when I tell you that you are fine are you to stop resting." He kissed her forehead. "Bridey and I would be lost without you."

She smiled, and he bet no one ever made her feel important to them. He'd have to remember the little things while courting her.

"I have to go and see if I can do the books or something for Parker. I will be back in a few minutes. Not enough time for you to get up and get into trouble."

"If you insist. I might even take a nap since I'm a lady of leisure."

The way her gaze followed him while he got ready to go made him hopeful. If she could find love in her heart, he'd be the happiest man on earth. Strange how he never craved love before, and now he couldn't do without it.

———

TWO DAYS LATER, Veronica stared at the book in her hand. She touched the front of it, the back of it, and even the first page. Her heart beat faster, and she wouldn't have been able to stop smiling if she wanted to.

"This is really for me?"

Max nodded. "I had Georgie get the book for you when she and Parker went into town yesterday."

She ran her fingers over the letters. The Mysterious Key and What it Opened, by Louisa May Alcott. "I can't wait to read it. A woman wrote it."

"Georgie was excited about that fact too. She wants to read it after you."

"You didn't have to buy me anything."

Max swallowed hard. "I wanted to get you something. I don't think you've had many gifts in your life."

"No, I haven't." She glanced down at her hands. "I think every gift I've been given except for Bridey has been from you. You are a nice man, Max. My heart feels like it's beating out of my chest."

"I hope that's a good thing." He stared into her eyes.

"Yes, you make me feel like I belong and that you care for me."

"I would think heart pounding would be more than just caring for you." He still stared.

"I don't know how to say what I mean. You make me smile, you make me happy, and you make my heart pound loudly." She turned from him. What was it he wanted her to say? She was so lacking in social or romantic ways.

Deep caring reflected in his eyes, but he said nothing.

"I feel so stupid," she murmured. "Other women know exactly how to flirt and attract a beau. I'm a disaster who has brought nothing but trouble with me. I wouldn't blame you if you walked away." Her eyes filled. She was a failure as a wife. He probably expected hot meals and things that involved her wifely duty. And no husband wanted a wife who wasn't pure. If she only had a way to make him happy. He'd been bringing her gifts. Why was he even bothering? She bowed her head wishing her feelings would just shut down. She learned not to show her hatred to Amis. Maybe she could learn to not show her budding feelings for Max.

Why were mail order bride marriages so popular? Max probably felt obligated to try to love her, but he was making *her* fall in love instead. Her life had become increasingly complicated.

"Veronica, are you all right?"

She nodded quickly. "I'm going to check on Bridey." She went into the bedroom and stared down at her beautiful daughter. She found love the instant she took Bridey in her arms. It had been surprising and the greatest blessing. Why would Max bother to bring her gifts if he wasn't trying to make their marriage a good one? He cared, she could tell he did, but did he love her?

She had to know. Veronica opened the bedroom door and walked until she stood in front of Max. She looked into his eyes. "Well, do you love me or not?"

His mouth dropped open, and that was all the answer she needed. Her heart hurt so suddenly she feared she would collapse at his feet. She couldn't let that happen, so she grasped her skirts and lifted them enough so she could run outside. She ran in a direction she wasn't familiar with, and when she was finally out of breath she sat down on a felled tree. She'd run out on Bridey again too. What was wrong with her?

She'd thought of herself as tough and able to handle whatever life threw at her. It had thrown more than its share her way, but she'd survived. Now she'd turned into the type of woman who hoped for a man's attentions. When had she turned into a pathetic female who thought life would be good?

Max made her feel too much, and now that he didn't return her feelings, she had no idea what she was supposed to do. After all they were married, but he could find himself someone he fancied better. She knew crops and everything about the growing nurturing and harvesting them. She knew about pigs and chickens. She didn't know about cattle or horses or men. Perhaps she should stick to what she knew.

She promised not to run again. She wished she could break that promise.

How was she supposed to face Max? She'd made such a fool of herself. Her cheeks heated and she touched them with her hands. Yes, they were indeed hot. Would he feel sorry for her? Poor Veronica thought he loved her. He was only being kind, and she needed to remember that. She'd have to keep her face blank and devoid of all feeling.

There was no use sitting anymore. Facing Max wouldn't go away. Standing, she began the walk back to her house. She had run very far. Suddenly, her fear of being so far from safety outweighed the humiliation of facing Max. Sighing, she walked faster. A movement in the corner of her eye froze her in place. Someone was in the woods to her right. She'd have to walk in a different direction; walking parallel to the woods wouldn't be wise.

Yet another unwise decision she'd made this day. She saw a few cowboys riding and waved them down. The one named Crumb lifted her up in front of him and he rode for home. He didn't ask, and she offered no explanation as to why she was out there.

Walter immediately lifted her down, and the porch and front door loomed large. It would only take one foot in front of the other. She was a coward, she'd gone to a promised beating easier than she was going to Max. A beating would eventually end, but not being loved would eat at her, she suspected. The thought of Bridey propelled her forward.

She opened the door and walked in. Her first instinct was to go and check on Bridey but Max had probably done that a few times already.

He stood as she entered and there was kindness in his eye. "I was worried about you."

"Someone was in the woods."

"The woods across from Parker's house?"

"No, the woods across the place they are building the houses for the freedmen."

"To the left or right?"

"To the left."

"You went that far? It's a long walk. You're lucky Crumb found you."

"You were watching out the window." Her voice was as toneless as she could manage.

"You never let me say anything before you took off." He took a step toward her. She put her hand up in front of her.

"I can't do this now, Max. I know nothing about feelings, and I realized that I spoke falsely. I've never known kindness, and I mistook your kindness for love, but they aren't the same thing. I know I love Bridey, and that is all I know."

He looked as though she'd slapped him. He stepped back, and a strange calm expression claimed his face. It must be a mask of some type. Had she hurt him with her words or was he angry with her? Maybe he really didn't care one way or the other.

Tears spilled down her face. If he didn't even care, she

wouldn't be able to take it. Why oh, why had she become so weak?

Max lifted her into his strong arms and sat on the sofa with her on his lap. "Please don't cry, sweetheart. I should have told you a while ago how much I love you. If you don't feel the same, that's fine. We get on well, and we both love Bridey. I think we have a good future together."

She buried her face into the crook of his neck. He loved her. Her heart opened, and it was as though a blessing itself was rushing into it. She pulled her head back so she could look into his eyes. "I felt like a fool. That's why I ran. I'm just a backward woman who knows nothing except for how to tend to crops. Gifts, trust, friendship, gentleness, and caring are all new to me. I had no idea if you were just being nice or if you cared for me, and I just blurted it out and then was too much a coward to hear your answer. I do love you Max. You're in my heart, and I feel like I could fly like a bird."

He cupped her head with his palm and then leaned down and kissed her. His lips were so gentle, and it felt as though his kiss was full of love. The tenderness turned into a bit of eagerness, and she enjoyed every minute of it. If this was what it would be like being a true wife to him, she'd have to stop trying to avoid it.

When the kiss was over, she sighed contentedly and laid her head on his shoulder. They were quiet for a long while. She was soaking in all the love. She'd missed so much in her life and now she was blessed with Max's love. She closed her eyes and silently thanked God.

CHAPTER ELEVEN

hen should he make his move? A few days later, Max sipped his coffee while he watched Veronica feed Bridey. He'd never felt so awkward before. He didn't want to rush things, but what if she was waiting? What if she expected to have their wedding night and he hadn't made a move?

Sometimes she was easy to read, but at other times, like this, he didn't have a clue and he had no one to ask. They'd just laugh and make jokes. He couldn't help but stare at her. It was like having a puzzle that wouldn't go together. He needed to figure it out.

Amis was still in town. In fact he never left town. He had a room at a boarding house, and if he wasn't there he was at the saloon. No one had a guess as to what he was really doing, but it made Max anxious. There were plenty of other towns he could stay in. Amis must know that Veronica was near.

Max had been tempted to go to town and buy Amis off, but people who were prone to lying couldn't be trusted. They'd looked through all the wanted posters, and the Sheriff said there would be more arriving today. Parker said he'd get someone to go by and get them.

Bridey was done feeding, and after Veronica burped her, she went to stand up with the baby in her arms. Max was right there to take Bridey.

"I'm completely healed, Max. In fact, I plan to make supper tonight. I'm not the best cook, but I'm certainly not the worst. Did you see the houses that are being built in the place they're calling Joy?" She smiled and shook her head. "Of course you have. I can see them from the porch."

It was good to know she was as nervous as he was. "The first few families will be moving in soon. It feels good to be able to help folks out."

"Too bad there aren't more like you and your army friends. The world could certainly do with some kindness. My life would have been so different if someone had offered a helping hand while I was growing up. People don't like poor people. I was always nice when I went to town, but I was glared at and once a man spat right in front of me."

He embraced both his wife and daughter in one big hug. "Those days are gone. People here like you. They don't care how you grew up. Plus you're with me, one of the greatest men ever."

"You sure are something," she teased.

They gazed into each other's eyes, and this time Max saw the longing Veronica had for him. It was a huge weight off his shoulders. At least he knew his touch would be welcome.

"I'll be at the corral if you need me. What are your plans today?"

"I plan to do laundry. Could you string some rope for me to hang the clothes on before you go?"

He kissed her cheek. "Consider it done." He kissed Bridey's forehead, and then he headed outside feeling buoyant. They were on the right track, and tonight just might be the night.

He strung the line for her and then headed to the barn.

"I swear he gets here later every day," Willis said.

"Kissing a wife goodbye must take a long time," Sandler said.

"Yes, that must be why he's tardy," Willis added.

"That's just jealousy talking," Max responded. He went to the bay he'd been working with.

"Dang right, we're jealous!" Sandler chuckled.

"Not me," Willis said with a smile.

"We'd best get busy. We have at least ten new cowhands coming soon, and we'll need the extra mounts." Max had the bay haltered and ready to go. "I think this one will be ready to learn to cut cattle and round up strays tomorrow."

"Good to hear, and since you're always late we can take the credit for all the hard work." Willis was laughing so hard he barely got the words out.

Smiling, Max kept walking right out of the barn.

VERONICA FOUND herself humming as she gathered the laundry. How strange. She wasn't the humming type. Happiness must be the reason. She had a lot to be happy about, and she was grateful. She put Bridey in a basket and brought her outside. The baby waved her little arms and smiled.

Life would be so different for Bridey than it had been for Veronica. She'd make sure of it. She glanced over to where Max was working with a brown horse. He was close enough she could see that he was pleased. Walter Green had nodded to her when she first came outside, but she didn't know where he went after that. Maybe the danger was over. Hopefully, Amis was gone for good.

Laundry was hard work, but hard work never bothered her. Finally, she got to the point where she didn't have to be bent over most of the time. She leaned back stretching her spine. She moved the basket with Bridey over to the clothes-line and went back to get the wet clothing.

She hung the first item and glanced at Bridey's basket with a big smile. Her smile faded, Bridey wasn't there. Panic hit, and she started shaking. She heard Bridey cry and listened again. It sounded as though her cry had come from inside the house.

Without hesitation, Veronica ran into the house fear clutched at her soul. Amis sat at the dining table with Bridey grasped between his hands.

Amis smiled. "I knew I'd find you, both you and my son. You are the lowest of low, woman. Just who do you think you are taking my child away? I planned to make you my wife, and you up and disappeared. I'm going to take little Amis here, and you too, since you're the one who feeds him. You are, aren't you?"

She nodded not taking her eyes off Bridey.

"I'll take you too, then. I might even marry you once we get back to Louisiana."

It took everything inside her not to show her disgust. Would he go crazy if she told him Bridey was a girl? It wasn't a chance she wasn't willing to take.

"Why don't you give me the baby?" she asked trying to smile.

"You takin' me for a fool? I'm holding on to my son."

Bridey started crying louder.

"He probably needs a diaper change. Here give him to me."

Amis narrowed his eyes. "Where do you change him?"

"In the bedroom." She clasped her hands together to hide their intense shaking.

Amis got up and walked into the bedroom with the baby. He came right back and pushed the baby at her. "Go, get my son changed."

Veronica walked near the window with Bridey.

"Trying to signal to someone? You think you can outsmart me, don't ya? As soon as we're away from here I'm going to teach you good for tryin' to defy me. Close those shutters and the curtains. I don't want anyone to see me." His harsh chuckle sent a chill over her. "At least I don't have to worry about that big man who has been watching the house. I have him all tied up." He feigned a lunge in her direction. "Get to it."

It was obvious from his superior tone that he thought he was so smart. Hopefully, Walter wasn't hurt. Veronica hurried and closed the shutters and curtains. Then she quickly took Bridey into the bedroom. Did he have a gun? She hadn't seen one, but Amis knew how to use his hands as weapons.

She left the door open. "Ew, little one what have you been eating?" she said loudly. "Amis, do you want to help? It's a loaded diaper!" Veronica held her breath hoping he'd say no.

"That's women's work. You ain't going to teach my boy any of those women chores either. I had some help, and I got in the crops. Made a bit of money, so here I am. Stan is watching over my piece of land. In fact, this was his idea and he was right. You have no right to take my son from me!"

From the sound of his voice he must be at the front door. It didn't sound as loud as it had earlier. Listening hard, she heard the door being latched. She laid Bridey on the bed and closed the bedroom door as silently as she could. Moving the wardrobe in front of it was very noisy though. She pushed as hard as she could and was almost to the door when he tried to charge in. With the last of her strength, she gave it one final shove and the door closed.

Amis began to howl in pain and then he used every bad word he knew. She must have initially closed it on some part of him. Bridey began to cry, but Veronica didn't dare move from the wardrobe. She had her back against it ready to push if needed.

She heard a strange sound and couldn't figure it out at first. But soon she recognized the sound of whittling. Amis must be using his bowie knife to make a hole in the door.

Please Max, please see the shutters.

It would take Amis a good while but it was possible that he'd get in.

"Go away!" she shouted.

"Never! You and my son belong to me!"

Should she tell him the baby was a girl? Would it make any difference? She looked at Bridey, who was crying harder. Her face had turned bright red. No, he might kill Bridey or even sell her. Where was Max? He must not have seen the signal. He might even be away on his horse. How long would she be able to hold Amis off?

The wardrobe inched toward her, and she tried to push it back against the door. It was exhausting work, and her strength began to ebb. He seemed to be winning and despair filled her. Would he wait until they left the house before he began to beat her? There was no where she could go. He'd just follow.

She pushed the wardrobe again with all her might when it came toward her so hard it hit her. The pain was almost unbearable but she gave it another try. Tears filled her eyes as she was woefully unsuccessful. Veronica dove for the bed and Bridey, but Amis got to the baby first.

He picked Bridey up none to gently and held her like a rag doll. She seemed all cried out.

"Give the baby back to me, Amis, please. I'll go with you just don't hurt the baby," she pleaded.

He grabbed Veronica's arm. "Oh, you're coming with me no matter what. I'm owed one wife and one son." He propelled her forward. "I have supplies hidden in the woods. Let's go."

"Diapers, did you bring diapers?" She held her breath hoping to stall.

"Hurry up and grab some. We need to get going and fast."

Bridey started crying again, and Veronica recognized the look in Amis' eyes. He was ready to hit someone. She had no doubt he'd hit Bridey. Veronica grabbed as many diapers as she could, jammed them into a bag and walked out the front door with Amis and Bridey.

"Keep your eyes facing forward. I don't want to alert anyone so just pretend we're going for a friendly walk."

"Give me the baby so she'll stop crying." Her heart raced. She'd called the baby "she." Had he noticed?

Amis hesitated for a moment and then handed Veronica the baby. It took a minute, but Bridey calmed. He said nothing, apparently not hearing her slip. She *must* be more careful.

"How are we getting to Louisiana?" Veronica asked.

"Walkin' mostly, I spent my money in town. It won't be so bad. We'll be home before winter."

"That long? We might as well get started." Veronica walked with him into the woods. All hope she had of someone seeing them were dashed. There had been no one in the yard. She took a shaky breath and put one foot in front of the other. If not for Bridey, Veronica would have gone numb from fear. It was usually better to think about other things when Amis was around.

They stopped near a big tree where two packs waited. They appeared heavy, and she'd be required to strap one to her back. Thank God she had healed.

Think of something else, Veronica. All she could think of was Psalm 71.

In thee, O Lord, do I put my trust: let me never be put to confusion.

Deliver me in thy righteousness, and cause me to escape: incline thine ear unto me, and save me.

Be thou my strong habitation, whereunto I may continually resort: thou hast given commandment to save me; for thou art my rock and my fortress.

Deliver me, O my God, out of the hand of the wicked, out of the hand of the unrighteous and cruel man.For thou art my hope, O Lord God: thou art my trust from my youth.

By thee have I been holden up from the womb: thou art he that took me out of my mother's bowels: my praise shall be continually of thee.

I am as a wonder unto many; but thou art my strong refuge.

Let my mouth be filled with thy praise and with thy honour all the day.

Cast me not off in the time of old age; forsake me not when my strength faileth.

For mine enemies speak against me; and they that lay wait for my soul take counsel together,

Saying, God hath forsaken him: persecute and take him; for there is none to deliver him.

O God, be not far from me: O my God, make haste for my help.

Let them be confounded and consumed that are adversaries to my soul; let them be covered with reproach and dishonour that seek my hurt.

But I will hope continually, and will yet praise thee more and more.

My mouth shall shew forth thy righteousness and thy salvation all the day; for I know not the numbers thereof.

I will go in the strength of the Lord God: I will make mention of thy righteousness, even of thine only.

O God, thou hast taught me from my youth: and hitherto have I declared thy wondrous works.

Now also when I am old and greyheaded, O God, forsake me not; until I have shewed thy strength unto this generation, and thy power to every one that is to come.

Thy righteousness also, O God, is very high, who hast done great things: O God, who is like unto thee!

Thou, which hast shewed me great and sore troubles, shalt quicken me again, and shalt bring me up again from the depths of the earth.

Thou shalt increase my greatness, and comfort me on every side.

I will also praise thee with the psaltery, even thy truth, O my God: unto thee will I sing with the harp, O thou Holy One of Israel.

My lips shall greatly rejoice when I sing unto thee; and my soul, which thou hast redeemed.

My tongue also shall talk of thy righteousness all the day long: for they are confounded, for they are brought unto shame, that seek my hurt.

Even though it was a prayer of protection for an old man, many of the words were what she felt. She became calmer as she remembered she never walked alone. God was always with her.

She put Bridey down on the grass as she hefted one of the packs onto her back. It was so heavy she almost fell over backwards. Grunting beneath her burden, she managed to bend with some difficulty and lift Bridey into her arms.

"How far are we going today?"

"You don't need to know. You just do what I say, understand?" He turned and glared at her.

"I understand," she said through gritted teeth.

A long while later, Bridey began to fuss, and Veronica was in such pain she thought her arms would fall off.

"I need to nurse the baby."

He ignored her, and they kept walking. Bridey fretted but didn't start full on crying. That lasted another good while.

"I need to feed the baby," she said a bit louder when Bridey began to squirm. Veronica held her breath when Amis suddenly stopped and turned.

"Feed my son and be quick about it." The impatience in his voice showered her in dread.

She put Bridey down, slipped off the pack, and sat on the ground. She unbuttoned her top and allowed Bridey to nurse. Amis watched, his eyes glittering with interest, and Veronica tensed up. Closing her eyes, she thought of Max and finally she calmed enough for her milk to flow.

"Does he always take this long?" Amis was grouchy.

"He's only about halfway done. I need to switch him to the other breast."

"Get to it. I don't have time to sit here all day." He licked his lips. "Greedy little thing, isn't he?"

"It'll make him big and strong," she said as steadily as she could.

"I know you didn't name him Amis. What do you call him?"

His question rattled her. "Br-Bradly. It's a good strong name."

"We could call him Junior. Amis Junior has a nice ring to it. His name is AJ for Amis Junior." Amis cocked his left brow as though he was expecting her to protest.

"AJ is fine." How many times would she have to give in to him and say it was fine? Was anyone looking for her yet? Grabbing a blanket she lay Bridey down. "I need to repack this. It's heavier on one side then the other."

Amis grunted and scratched himself in a place that sickened her. Veronica unpacked the cans of food and all the cooking supplies including a bag of coffee beans. Maybe she could leave a trail of coffee beans? It couldn't hurt. She scooped some out of the bag and filled her pockets. After she repacked the bag, she strapped it on her back again and picked up Bridey and the blanket. The blanket would serve to keep them both warm.

If no one found her, she'd probably be dead before she got to Louisiana. Neither she nor Bridey had warm clothes on. As they continued to hike, Veronica dropped a coffee bean every so often. Tomorrow, she'd figure some way to make a sling for Bridey to lie in. It would help the pain in her arms.

On and on they went. Amis refused to stop when Bridey's diaper became wet. Now it was sopping and so was Veronica. Finally, Veronica took the diaper off and left it on the ground. A wet diaper wasn't good for a baby.

They came to a clearing late in the day and Amis took off his pack and sat down. "You'll need wood for a fire and you'll also need to fetch water. I'll hold my son."

A shiver went down Veronica's spine. "Let me just put a diaper on the baby."

"What happened to the one he was wearin'?"

"I had to take it off. It was so wet I was afraid of a rash." She set Bridey down on the blanket and used her baby gown as a cover so Amis would not get a clear view as she fished a diaper out of the pack. Quickly Veronica put the diaper on, relieved she had done so without revealing that Bridey was a girl.

"Where is it?"

She knew that tone of voice. She stood, leaving Bridey on the blanket, and took a few steps away so she wouldn't be hurt. Veronica braced herself but nothing could help against the strong slap he gave her. Gingerly, she touched her cheek, but he wasn't done. He back handed her on the other side of her face.

"I'd forgotten how dim witted you are. Someone could

find the diaper and then try to track us." He hit her again knocking her to the ground.

She tried to stay quiet, but she screamed at the last slap. Tears filled her eyes. He was just warming up.

"If I'm too hurt, I won't be able to walk tomorrow."

"You'll walk when I tell you to walk." He kicked her lower back and stomped away, muttering about having to get the wood.

Veronica went to Bridey's side and stroked her cheek. If she could, she'd grab her and make a run for it but she wouldn't get very far. The pain in her back was beyond anything she'd felt before. She'd need the night to rest it. She was in trouble, real trouble.

CHAPTER TWELVE

*M*ax rode the horse back to the corral and immediately spotted the closed shutters. He was on the ground running before the horse came to a stop. His gut clenched as he opened the door to his house and found it empty with signs of a struggle near the bedroom door.

Running back out, he yelled to Sandler and Willis. "Where's Green? Veronica and my daughter are gone!"

"I'll check Parker's house," Sandler shouted as he ran.

"I'll check the bunkhouse and other out buildings," Willis yelled over his shoulder.

Max stood in the middle of the yard with his fists clenched. He needed to check if anything was gone from the house. He went in and looked around. The bedroom door had been destroyed and the wardrobe had been moved. Veronica's coat still hung on a hook. He opened the shutters and all he could see was the clothes she had hung out to dry, blowing in the wind.

Amis had taken her. There was no other explanation, and he was going to wring that man's neck when he caught him!

Max went out to the porch and started looking for signs, trampled grass, footprints, something dropped. There was a path of broken grass headed toward the forest. He waved to Sandler who nodded. Then he saw Willis helping Green walk toward Parker's house. He didn't look to have any bullet or knife wounds, no obvious visible bleeding, but it was hard to tell from the distance between them.

Sandler spoke to Willis for a brief moment before he hurried toward Max. "He clobbered Green over the head and left him behind your house. I see you found their trail. Looks to me like it was just a man—probably Amis—and Veronica; he didn't bother to bring help." Sandler turned toward Parker's house and signaled that there was one man.

"They'll bring supplies. Let's get going." Max didn't want to delay any longer. He and Sandler kept their eyes on the ground as they walked further into the woods. Max signaled for them to stop.

"Look here. He must have had his supplies here," Max said as he studied the area.

"Looks like they stopped here for a bit," Sandler remarked. "The baby was laid there," he pointed to an imprint on the ground."

Max pointed in a westerly direction. "They went that way, and look how much deeper Veronica's steps are. She must be carrying supplies. That should slow them down a bit."

Both men turned when they heard Parker and Green join them.

"You all right, Green? You can sit this one out," Max said as he looked at the lump on the side of Green's head.

"I'm fine. Let's get your girls back." Green offered a shaky smile. "I get to hit Amis first."

Parker and Green had supplies with them and both Max and Sandler eased Green of the burden of carrying anything. They followed the path until they got to the dirty diaper.

"We know we're trailing the right people," Parker said.

"It's a good sign. Both Veronica and Bridey must be fine. Amis wouldn't have changed the diaper," Green said.

"Good point." Max kept following the trail. He bent over wondering what the brown beans were. And then he smiled. His wife was good, very good. He nodded at the trail. "Coffee beans leading us to them."

"Good on Veronica. She's keeping her head during all this." Sandler nodded.

They followed the beans, and Max signaled for them to stop. Amis was sitting against a tree holding the baby while Veronica was starting a fire. She turned her head and he saw the marks on her face. Rage coursed through him. Amis had better not have forced himself on her. After a moment, Max set the thought aside. He needed a cool head if the rescue was to go as they needed it to.

Parker looked the situation over and signaled their plan to them. Each man got into position. They were basically surrounding Amis.

They waited a long while. They wanted Amis, but not while he had Bridey in his arms. Veronica got the fire started and put a pot over it. Amis held Bridey out to her, and she grabbed a clean diaper before she took her. She walked a bit away from Amis before she put Bridey down to change her.

At the sound of Parker's bird call, they all closed in with their guns drawn.

With a startled cry, Amis struggled to stand, his eyes darting frantically about the clearing.

Rage threatened to overtake Max again, and he had to hold himself back. He wanted to pound Amis good. But Parker was able to tie the disgusting piece of filth up without incident.

Max turned and looked at his wife and daughter. His heart hurt for Veronica, and he immediately went to her side.

"I'm fine and so is Bridey. It was frightening, but I knew you'd come for us." Tears trailed down her cheek. Her very red cheek.

Max held them both to him, rocking back and forth, and then he drew away slightly and cupped his hand under Veronica's chin. He turned her head one way and then the other. Dark bruises were forming, but he squashed his anger. "Did he... Did he—?"

Veronica tried to smile but ended up wincing instead. "He didn't get a chance. I'm so glad you're here. He took Bridey while I was hanging the laundry, and then I ran into the house. He was there."

"It looked like you put up a good fight with the wardrobe. I'm sorry I wasn't there to see the shutters closed." Guilt invaded him.

"There's no use going back over things you can't change. He still doesn't know that Bridey is a girl. I was afraid he'd throw her away or hurt her or..."

Max put his arm around Veronica and walked closer to Amis. Then he kissed Veronica's forehead and took Bridey into his arms. Bridey smiled at him.

"If you ever come near my wife and daughter again you'll be sorry."

Amis' eyes opened wide. "What do you mean *daughter*?"

Veronica crossed her arms and took a step forward. "Yes, a daughter. Her name is Bridey. I do not owe it to you to be your wife because my sister died. You forced yourself on me time and again. I didn't want you and you knew that. This is *my* daughter! She belongs to my husband and me. You are nothing to us and you never will be. You are nothing but a drunken fool." She stepped back and leaned on Max's arm."

"So you like to force women, do you?" Parker asked.

138

"Max, why don't you take your family home. We'll deal with Amis here. Don't worry, he won't bother you again."

Max held Bridey in one arm and took Veronica's hand. They walked to the path and kept walking until they came to his horse.

GEORGIE WAS SITTING on their front porch. "Oh, thank goodness. I was so worried. I have water heating for a bath and I have herbs." She blushed and lowered her voice. "I have herbs for if he abused you."

"Come on inside," Max invited.

He led Veronica to the sofa and put Bridey into her arms. He glanced at Veronica and then at Georgie. "I'll give you ladies time to talk."

As soon as he left, Georgie sat by her side. "Did he force you? Oh, my, your face will be black and blue by morning. It must hurt something awful. I have willow bark tea ready for you."

Veronica patted her friend's hand. "He slapped me around a bit, but thank God he didn't get a chance to do more harm. I'd love some of the tea. My face and back hurt."

Georgie got up and poured the tea. Despite the pain, Veronica was happy. She was grateful. She had a friend; a real friend. It felt amazing to know that she was liked by another woman. It warmed her heart and made her feel worthy somehow.

She hugged her daughter, and when Max walked back in, her heart was near to overflowing. She had a family and friends. *Thank you Lord, for hearing my plea and thank you for your many blessings.*

CHAPTER THIRTEEN

*M*ax came up behind her while she was cooking and wrapped his arms around her waist. He kissed the side of her neck, and she shivered.

"You're face looks lovely," he whispered.

"The bruising is gone, finally."

"Did you notice that Bridey doesn't wake up in the middle of the night anymore?"

"Yes, I noticed." At one time, she would have been afraid of where the conversation was going, but Max's love made her feel different.

"I want to ask you something, my love, but I want you to know that if you're not—."

"Yes!" She turned in his arms and faced him. "I want to make this marriage real. I want to be in your arms. I want to be with you tonight." She felt his body shiver against hers.

"I love you with all my heart, Veronica. Both you and Bridey. I'm the luckiest man I know. I think it was more than just chance that you saw my ad in the newspaper. I like to think that God had a hand in our union."

"I love you too, Max, so very much. I used to pray to be

away from Amis, and nothing happened. But God answered my prayers just in His own time." She trembled. "And if He had taken me away from Amis earlier, then Bridey—" Emotion choked her, and she couldn't finish her thought.

"I love you." Max kissed her so tenderly she thought she'd cry from the beauty of it. "I'll meet you in bed a little after dark."

She laughed. "We meet there anyway."

He grinned and gave her a wink. "Don't be late." He let her go and went back to work.

Veronica couldn't stop smiling. Her husband was funny and charming and handsome and best of all he loved both her and Bridey. Max had healed her heart and her shattered trust. She wasn't afraid to go to her husband now. She felt both serene and filled with anticipation. The fear was gone.

She never thought she'd ever completely trust another man again. Up until she arrived at the town of Spring Water she never really knew an honorable man. Knowing that there was no help for her made it worse. How can the law think of a wife as the husband's property to do what he wishes? How could whole communities turn a blind eye because they considered it a family matter? Surviving the War Between the States had been hard enough but to have the extra burden of being abused by Amis had almost been her undoing. She had grown strong and she had grown wise. She'd never allow another to hit her again. Veronica smiled. With Max she wouldn't even have to worry about it.

She took a deep breath. She was part of a wonderful community that was growing and she couldn't wait to see the changes. Hopefully they could build a church and a school and she couldn't wait for the freedmen to move their families onto the ranch. It was time for rebuilding lives, not cutting them short. It was through the grace of God that she saw Max's advertisement in the newspaper.

Her eyes misted. God hadn't forgotten her after all. He was waiting for the right man for her. She had faith she would be blessed with Max's children. Somehow she knew both she and Max would still be around to see their children's children.

She hoped Max's friends Sandler and Willis eventually found wives of their own. The bet had hurt but now she was glad. It had led her to her loving and tender husband. God sure worked miracles.

ABOUT THE AUTHOR

Sexy Cowboys and the Women Who Love Them...
Finalist in the 2012 and 2015 RONE Awards.
Top Pick, Five Star Series from the Romance Review.
Kathleen Ball writes contemporary and historical western
romance with great emotion and
memorable characters. Her books are award winners and
have appeared on best sellers lists including: Amazon's Best
Seller's List, All Romance Ebooks, Bookstrand, Desert
Breeze Publishing and Secret Cravings Publishing Best
Sellers list. She is the recipient of eight Editor's Choice
Awards, and The Readers' Choice Award for Ryelee's
Cowboy.
Winner of the Lear diamond award Best Historical Novel-
Cinders' Bride
There's something about a cowboy

facebook.com/kathleenballwesternromance
twitter.com/kballauthor
instagram.com/author_kathleenball

So Many Roads to Choose

The Settlers

Greg

Juan

Scarlett

Mail Order Brides of Spring Water

Tattered Hearts

Shattered Trust

Glory's Groom

Battered Soul

Romance on the Oregon Trail

Cora's Courage

Luella's Longing

Dawn's Destiny

Terra's Trial

Candle Glow and Mistletoe

The Kabvanagh Brothers

Teagan: Cowboy Strong

Quinn: Cowboy Risk

Brogan: Cowboy Pride

Sullivan: Cowboy Protector

Donnell: Cowboy Scrutiny

Murphy: Cowboy Deceived

Fitzpatrick: Cowboy Reluctant

Angus: Cowboy Bewildered

The Greatest Gift

Love So Deep

Luke's Fate

Whispered Love

Love Before Midnight

I'm Forever Yours

Finn's Fortune

Glory's Groom

55606570R00093